Man on a Leash

Charles Williams

MAN ON A LEASH

G. P. Putnam's Sons
New York

Man on a Leash

I

DAWN was just breaking when he pulled into town after the late-night drive from San Francisco, and it would be hours yet before officialdom was astir. A boy in an all-night service station worried the spattered insects off his windshield while the tank was being filled and told him how to find the cemetery. It was about two miles south of the city limits, he said, and if he wondered why an out-of-state license wanted to visit Coleville's burying ground at this strange hour, he made no mention of it.

Romstead wasn't sure himself, since he had no flowers to deposit on the grave and would have felt too uncomfortable and self-conscious in such a lavender gesture anyway, knowing the Rabelaisian laughter this would have evoked in the departed. Maybe he simply had to see the grave before he could accept it.

Certainly Sergeant Crowder's few facts over the telephone had sounded as improbable as a bad television script, and the big stud was indestructible anyway. Nobody who'd survived waterfront brawls, typhoons, picket-line battles, a lifetime of exuberant and extramarital wenching, torpedoings, western ocean gales, and fourteen months on the Murmansk run in World War II could have got himself killed in this plastic desert town on the edge of nowhere. And not merely killed, Crowder had said, but executed.

"Six ten," the boy said. Romstead passed him the credit card. He made out the slip, imprinted it with the card, and

1

then broke stride, looking up suddenly as the name struck him in the midst of this boring and automatic routine. He seemed about to say something but changed his mind, filled in the license number, and passed the clipboard in through the window. Romstead signed and drove out.

The business district was only six or eight blocks, with traffic lights at three of the intersections. South of it were several motels, all showing vacancy signs, a residential area of modest houses and green lawns, and then a highway maintenance depot and some oil storage tanks. For a mile or so beyond the city limits there were small irrigated farms on both sides of the highway, but after the blacktop climbed a slight grade out of the valley, he was in open rangeland again. Almost immediately he saw the cemetery ahead of him and slowed.

It was on the slope of a rocky hillside to the right, with a row of stunted cedars along the fence in front and a pair of fieldstone pillars framing the entrance. He pulled off and stopped, and when he cut the engine and got out, he was aware of profound silence and the odor of sage. It was full daylight now, the sky washed with pink and gold above the waste of flinty hills and desert scrub to the east, while to westward the thrusting escarpments of the Sierra stood out sharply in the clear desert air. The cooling engine made a loud ticking sound in the hush, and miles overhead an invisible jet drew its contrail across the sky. He sighed and shook his head as he walked over to the entrance. It was a hell of a morning to be dead.

The iron grillwork gates were closed but not locked. Then, when he was already inside and walking slowly up the avenue between the rows of graves, it suddenly occurred to him there was no way to identify it when he found it. There wouldn't be any headstone yet. How could there be, since

2

he was the only one to place an order, and he hadn't even known about it until eight hours ago?

But surprisingly there was one. Just ahead and to his left was the raw mound of a new grave, the only one in sight from here, and when he approached, he saw the simple inscription chiseled into the granite slab at the head of it:

GUNNAR ROMSTEAD

1906–1972

He walked over and stood looking down at this final resting place of what had possibly been the world's most improbable parent, not quite sure what his feelings were. There was no profound sense of grief or loss, certainly, for a man he'd seen so few times in his life. It was more a sense of wonder, he thought, at all that vast energy's having been stilled at last or the incongruity of prosaic burial in a country cemetery so far from the sea when anything less than a Viking funeral pyre would have been an anticlimax.

Mayo had asked him once about his relationship with his father. The question had surprised him, for he hadn't even thought about it in years, and now that he did the best answer he could give her was that aside from mutual respect, he didn't think there had ever been any. From the onset of puberty both had grown up in a totally male environment where self-sufficiency was a prerequisite to survival—the one at sea and the other in a succession of military schools and the locker rooms of college jocks—so it would never have occurred to either of them that young men really needed anybody. As a girl, of course, she couldn't believe this or understand it, and he had despaired of trying to explain it to her.

He stood for another minute or two, his face impassive, feeling somehow lacking that there didn't seem to be any-

3

thing to say or do. Then he lifted one hand in a slight gesture that might have been a farewell and turned and walked back to the car. The sun was coming up now, and he remembered the line from Ecclesiastes. A hamfisted ex-jock quoting the Preacher, he thought; the old man would say he'd gone fruit.

Executed? What in hell had Crowder meant by that? And by whom? Then he shook his head impatiently. Racking his brains was a sheer waste of time until he could talk to somebody who had the answers. He drove back to town.

He'd better get a place to stay. The chances were he'd be here all day, and he should try to get some sleep before he made the drive back. Upcoming on the right was the Conestoga Motel, which seemed as likely a prospect as any. He swung in and stopped under the porte cochere in front of the office. Beyond the glass wall a row of slot machines lay in wait for the tourist with the patient inevitability of snares in a game trail, and a woman with blue-white hair sipped coffee and flipped through a newspaper at the desk. She looked up with a smile as he entered. Yes, there was a vacancy.

"And a king-size bed, if you'd like one," she added, with a not entirely objective appraisal of his size.

"Fine." He began filling in the registration card while she plucked a key from the pigeonholes behind her.

"How long will you be staying, Mr.—"

"Romstead," he replied. "Just one day, probably."

"Oh." As the boy in the service station had, she glanced up sharply and appeared on the point of saying something, but did not. "I see." The smile was still there, but something had gone out of it; it was now straight out of the innkeeper's manual. He passed over the American Express card, wondering at this seemingly unanimous response to the name around here. Well, the old man had never been one to blush unseen, even in larger places than Coleville, and whatever

4

his hangups might have been, awe of community opinion wasn't one of them.

He signed the slip and went out with the key. Room 17 was on the ground floor at the rear of the U which enclosed the standard small swimming pool and sun deck with patio furniture and umbrellas. Several of the cars parked before the units were being loaded now as travelers prepared to hit the road again.

The day's heat was beginning, but the room was cool, dim behind the heavy green drapes, smelled faintly of some aerosol gunk masquerading as fresh air, and was wholly interchangeable with a million others along the concrete river. He dropped the bag on a luggage rack and switched on a light. Sitting on the side of the bed, he reached for the thin directory beside the telephone. It covered the whole county, rural subscribers and the other small towns in addition to Coleville, but there was no Gunnar Romstead in it, no Romstead of any kind. Unlisted phone, he thought. The yellow pages revealed there were two mortuaries in town, but no monument works or stonecutter. The stone no doubt had come from Reno then, but he could probably find out from the sheriff's office and see if there were any accounts to settle.

He shaved and showered and came out of the bath scrubbing himself vigorously with the towel, a heavyset figure of a man with haze-gray eyes, big, beat-up hands, and an allover leathery tan except for a narrow strip about his middle. He ran a comb through the sun-streaked blond hair without noticeably improving an indifferent haircut, shrugged, and tossed the comb back into the toilet kit.

He put on slacks and sport shirt. It was only a short walk to the center of town; there was no need to take the car. He went up the sidewalk under the increasing weight of the sun, accustomed to it and scarcely noticing it but aware at the same time of the unfamiliar dryness of the air and the faint odors of dust and sage. Not many of the places of business were open yet, and the pace was unhurried along the street.

Just ahead was a coffee shop with a couple of newspaper vending racks in front. One of them held the San Francisco Chronicle. He fished in his pocket and was about to drop in the coins when he saw it was yesterday's; it was too early yet for today's. Something half forgotten nudged the edges of his mind as he went inside and ordered coffee. What was it? And where? Then he remembered, and grinned, but with a faint tightness in his throat.

It was in New York. He'd got permission from the military academy he attended in Pennsylvania to come down to meet his father for a day while his ship was in port. They'd had lunch somewhere, and afterward out on the sidewalk his father had flagged a taxi to take them to the ball game at Yankee Stadium. As it was pulling to the curb, he dropped a coin in a vending machine for a newspaper. There was no sign on it warning that it was out of order, but it refused to open, and punching the coin return was of no avail. It didn't work either. Passersby turned to gawk at this familiar scene of man's being bilked by another complacent, nickel-grabbing machine, and while somebody else might have given it a shake and retreated muttering, his father stepped back, calmly shoved a size-12 English brogue through the glass front, lifted out his paper, folded it under his arm, and strolled over to the cab while he, Eric, watched aghast in his cadet's uniform. By the time he'd got into the cab and they pulled away his father was already immersed in the financial section, and when he ventured some doubt about the legality of this direct action, the old man had looked up, puzzled.

"What? Oh— Son, never expect anything free in this world;

6

you pay for everything you get. But at the same time make sure they give you every goddamned thing you pay for."

The sheriff's office was on the ground floor at the rear of the new courthouse and city hall, a long room with a wide double doorway. A blond girl came out carrying a sheaf of papers and nodded as he went in. There was a railing just inside, and beyond it five or six desks and banks of filing cabinets. At the back of the room were two barred windows and a door that presumably led to the alley and the parking area for official cars. From an open doorway into another room at the left there issued the sound of static and the short, staccato bursts of police-band voices. There was a corridor at the right end of the room, and next to it a bulletin board, a case containing shotguns and rifles, and a small table holding a percolator and some coffee cups. A dark-haired man of about thirty was typing at one of the desks near the railing. He got up and came over.

"Good morning. Can I help you?"

"I'd like to speak to the sheriff," Romstead replied. "Is he in yet?"

"No. He's got to go to court today; he may not be in at all. But if it's a complaint, I can take it. My name's Orde."

"No complaint," Romstead said. "It's about Captain Romstead."

"And you are?"

"Eric Romstead. He was my father."

There was no reaction this time unless it was the total lack of any expression at all, which was probably professional. Romstead went on, "There was a wire from your office. I called last night from San Francisco and talked to a man named Crowder."

"Yeah. Well, Crowder doesn't come on till four, but the man you want to see is Brubaker, chief deputy. He's in charge of the case. Just a minute."

7

He went back to his desk and spoke into the phone. He replaced the instrument and nodded. "Just have a seat there. He'll be with you in a couple of minutes."

There was a bench along the wall beside the doors. Romstead sat down. A teletype clattered briefly in the communications room. Orde lit a cigarette and stared at the form in his typewriter.

"What happened anyway?" Romstead asked.

"Didn't Crowder tell you?"

"Just that he'd been shot. Executed is the word he used."

"Crowder watches a lot of TV." Orde leaned back in the swivel chair and dropped the book of matches onto the desk. "But then I guess you can't argue with it, even if it is a little Hollywood. He was found on the city dump, shot in the back of the head. I'm sorry."

"But for Christ's sake, who did it?"

"We don't know. Except that it was real professional and some action he brought here with him. We could have done without it."

This made no sense at all, of course, and Romstead was about to point it out but did not. He'd come this far to get the facts from somebody who knew what he was talking about, so he could wait a few more minutes. At that moment the door opened at the rear of the room, and a white-hatted deputy came in, ushering ahead of him an emaciated middle-aged man whose face was covered with a stubble of graying whiskers. The latter looked around once with an expression that managed to be sly and hangdog at the same time and then down at the floor as he shuffled forward when the deputy released his arm and gestured toward the chair by Orde's desk. "Park it, Wingy."

"Not again?" Orde asked.

"Again," the deputy replied.

The prisoner sat down, still looking at the floor, and began

8

to pat his clothing for nonexistent cigarettes. Orde tossed the pack across the desk.

"Who'd he unveil it for this time?" he asked. "The League of Women Voters?"

"Rancher's wife out on the Dennison road." The deputy sighed and went over to the table to pour a cup of coffee. "I wish to Christ I had one I was that proud of."

The prisoner was now patting his pockets for matches. Orde tossed him the book. "Here." He shook his head as he rolled a new form into his typewriter and spoke in the tone of one addressing a wayward child.

"Wingy, someday you're going to wave that lily at some woman's got a cleaver in her hand, and she's going to chop it off and stuff it in your ear."

A phone rang. Orde punched a button on the desk and answered it. "Okay," he said. He looked over at Romstead and gestured toward the corridor. "That was Brubaker. Second door on the left."

"Thanks." Romstead let himself in through the gate in the railing and went up the hallway. The door was open. It was a small office. Brubaker was at the desk with his back to a closed venetian blind, removing the contents of a thick manila folder. He stood up and held out his hand, a heavy, florid-faced man with spiky red hair graying at the temples. The handshake was brusque and his manner businesslike, but he smiled briefly as he waved toward the chair in front of the desk.

"You're a hard man to get hold of." He sat down, picked up his cigar from a tray on the desk, and leaned forward to study the material from the envelope. "We've been trying to run you down for two weeks."

"I was out of town," Romstead said. "I just got back last night."

"I know. We got your address from your father's attorney.

9

We kept trying to call you and finally asked the San Francisco police to check your apartment. The manager said he didn't know where you were. Crowder's note here says you were on a boat somewhere. You a seaman, too?"

"No," Romstead replied. "Just some cruising and fishing in the Gulf of California. A friend of mine had a motor-sailer down there, and we brought it back to San Diego. I flew up to San Francisco last night, and your wire was waiting for me along with the other mail."

"So you were on this boat at the time? Where?"

"If it was two weeks ago, we'd have been somewhere around Cape San Lucas."

"Where's that?"

"The southern tip of Baja California."

"I see. What do you do for a living?"

"Nothing at the moment. I've been in Central America for the past twelve years but sold my business there about four months ago."

"And what was that?"

"Boats. I had the distributorship in Costa Rica for a line of fiber glass powerboats—runabouts, fishermen, cruisers, and so on."

"And when's the last time you saw your father?"

"About four years ago. I came up to Southern California to visit the plant, and his ship was in Long Beach. I went aboard, and we had a couple of drinks."

"The two of you sure as hell didn't live in each other's pockets, did you? You didn't know he had an apartment in San Francisco?"

Romstead shook his head. "I didn't even know he'd retired or that he'd bought a place here until I talked to Crowder last night. I wrote to him in care of the steamship company when I sold out and came up to San Francisco, and I guess they forwarded the letter. He hardly ever wrote at all; I'd get a card from him once or twice a year, and that was about it. But just how did it happen? And have you got any leads at all as to who did it?"

"No. We were hoping you might be able to help us, but if you didn't keep in any closer touch than that—"

"What about identification?"

"No problem." Brubaker gave an impatient wave of the hand. "What the hell—a man six feet five with snow-white hair? Anyway, his stuff was still in his wallet. But just for the record you might as well verify it."

Romstead mentally braced himself and took the two large glossies Brubaker held out. The first was a full-length view of a man lying on his back in a sordid litter of trash: empty bottles, newspapers, a headless doll, charred magazines, and rusting cans, and beyond him, just above the rumpled mane of white hair, a burst sofa cushion and some twisted and half-rotted shoes. It was his father. He was clad in a dark suit, light shirt, and tie, and his ankles were hobbled with a short length of rope. His hands and forearms were under him, twisted behind his back. There were no visible signs of violence except that there was something in his mouth and on his face.

The second was a close-up, just the head and shoulders, taken in the same location. The eyes were open, staring blankly upward with the dry and faintly dusty look of death. The mouth was spread wide, apparently having been pulled open while the substance, whatever it was, was poured in until it overflowed in a small mound. It looked like flour or confectioners' sugar. There was more of it in the nostrils and on the chin and some on the ground on each side of the face. Romstead's eyes were bleak as he pushed the two photos together and handed them back.

"That's him. But what is that stuff in his mouth?"

"Lactose," Brubaker said. "We had it analyzed."

11

"Lactose?"

"More commonly known as milk sugar."

"But why? Some psychopath's idea of good clean fun?"

"Oh, the message seems to be clear enough, but why us? We're just old country boys."

"I think you've lost me," Romstead said.

"Don't you know what they use it for?"

"No—" Romstead began. Then he gestured impatiently. "Oh, for Christ's sake!"

"Exactly. To cut heroin. I'd say he tried to burn somebody, only he did it to the wrong crowd."

"What the hell kind of pipe dream is this? He never touched the stuff in his life. He was a shipmaster."

"I know that. But how many retired ship captains you ever hear of—or any other working stiff on a salary—that managed to save a million dollars?"

II

ROMSTEAD stared in disbelief. "Million dollars? He didn't have anything like that."

"You don't seem to know anything about your father at all."

"Oh, I don't doubt he was pretty well fixed for his retirement—but not these boxcar figures you're talking about."

"Listen!" Brubaker picked another sheet out of the file and scanned it for what he sought. "On July twelfth, just two days before he wound up on the city dump here, he went into his bank on Montgomery Street in San Francisco and drew out two hundred and fifty thousand dollars—"

"What?"

"In cash. Said he needed it for a business deal. Now you tell me what kind of business transaction you need currency for."

Romstead sighed. "Okay, the whole thing's crazier than hell, but go on."

"Right. Early in the morning of July fourteenth two men on a garbage truck found his body there. Two of us went out first and then called the county coroner. Your father's wallet was still in one of the inside pockets of his coat, with all his identification in it and about forty dollars in cash. His legs were hobbled together with that rope so he could walk but not run, and his hands were bound behind him with two-inch adhesive tape. He was still a powerful man for his age—

13

sixty-six, wasn't it?—but a gorilla couldn't have broken that tape the way they had it wound on there.

"As soon as we started digging that lactose out of his mouth, we found that his lower lip was cut, one lower incisor was broken, and the one next to it was gone altogether. We'd already found the entrance wound in the back of the head, of course— You want all this medical who-struck-John about the trajectory?"

"No. Just a rough translation."

"What it amounted to was that the bullet had entered fairly high up in the back of the head and exited through the rear part of the palate and on out the mouth. As tall as he was, it meant that unless the gunman was standing on a stepladder, your father was on his knees. It doesn't show in the pictures, but there was some carbon on the knees of his pants from those charred magazines, and there was another, secondary wound on top of his head, the scalp split open as if he'd been hit with something.

"The ground was too hard and there'd already been too many people milling around to make out any tracks, but the logical supposition was that he'd been taken out of a car, duck-walked over to the edge of the dump, slugged and knocked to his knees, and then held while he was shot in the back of the head like a Chinese execution. A real homey crowd. Could have been two of 'em, or three, or even more. We started sifting the place and found tooth fragments and finally the slug itself. It was too beat-up for any chance of ever matching it to any particular gun, but we could arrive at the caliber. It was a thirty-eight, which of course is no help at all; there are thousands of 'em everywhere.

"We're pretty sure he must have been blindfolded when they took him out there, and then they removed it because it was something that might possibly be traced. He was too big a bull to go quietly when he saw where they were taking him; there'd have been some bruises and torn clothing and plowed-up scenery before they ever got him there, even tied up the way he was."

Brubaker paused to relight his cigar. He puffed and dropped the match in the ashtray. Romstead winced, trying to push the too-vivid scene out of his mind. "When did he leave here?" he asked.

"Nobody knows for sure. He lived out there alone and came and went as he pleased and seldom told anybody anything—though I wouldn't bet there weren't a few women around here could fill in a lot more blanks than they'll ever admit. Your old man must have been one hell of a swordsman when he was younger—say only around sixty—and from what I gather, he hadn't slowed down a great deal.

"Sometimes he drove to San Francisco, and sometimes he just went over to Reno and took the plane. We checked the airlines, and they have no record of a reservation for him any time in July at all, so he must have driven all the way. As far as we can pin it down, the last time he was seen here was on the Fourth, when he had his car serviced at his usual place, the Shell station on Aspen Street.

"When he planned to be gone more than a few days, he usually made arrangements with a kid named Wally Pruitt to go out to the place and check on it now and then, make sure the automatic sprinklers were working, and so on, but this time Wally says he didn't call him, so apparently he wasn't intending to stay long when he left or else he just forgot—"

The phone rang. "Excuse me," Brubaker said, and picked it up. "Brubaker. . . . Oh, good morning. . . . Yeah, he did. As a matter of fact, he's here in my office right now. . . . Okay, I'll tell him. You're welcome."

15

He hung up. "That was your father's lawyer, Sam Bolling. He's been trying to get hold of you, too, and he'd like to see you as soon as we're through here."

"Right," Romstead said. "Thanks."

"His office is in the Whittaker Building at Third and Aspen. It was through Sam, as a matter of fact, that we first learned about the money and also that your father had an apartment in San Francisco. He's the executor of the estate, and as soon as he learned Captain Romstead was dead, he notified the tax people, the banks, any possible creditors, all that legal bit. The bank in San Francisco told him about that whopping withdrawal, and he immediately notified us. He was worried about the money, of course, but we already had a pretty good idea nobody was ever going to find it.

"We asked the San Francisco police to check out his apartment while we searched the house here to see if we could turn up any trace of it just on the off chance he still hadn't consummated the so-called deal. There was no money in either place, but we did find evidence of just about what we expected—or that is, San Francisco did. All we found in the house was a thousand Havana cigars stashed in a closet. But the apartment was the payoff.

"It had just been thoroughly cleaned, with the exception of one item he overlooked. In a closet there was an empty suitcase that had some white powder spilled in the lining. The police vacuumed it and had the stuff analyzed. It was heroin, all right, and it had been cut with milk sugar.

"So there you are. All the evidence says he must have been mixed up in smuggling junk when he was going to sea and still had connections. Somebody brought in a consignment for him, he drew out that money to pay for it, but before he sold it as pure heroin to the next bunch of bastards along the pipeline, he cut it, or cut part of it, to increase the take. Sound business procedure, I suppose, as long as you don't

16

do it to the wrong people. He apparently did, and they caught up with him after he got back here."

"No," Romstead said. "I don't buy it. Maybe in a lot of ways he wouldn't qualify as Husband of the Year or the thoroughly domesticated house pet, but junk—no."

"I wouldn't call you an expert witness," Brubaker pointed out. "You've practically admitted you didn't know a damn thing about where he was or what he was doing."

"No, but I don't see that you've got any evidence, anyway. Who says that suitcase was his? You know as well as I do he wasn't using that apartment alone. Christ, with his track record there could have been a half dozen girls in and out of it at one time or another, any one of 'em a possible junkie or with a junkie boyfriend on the side."

"And I suppose he was just keeping those forty boxes of Upmann cigars for some girl? Maybe she didn't want her mother to know she smoked."

Romstead gestured impatiently. "Cigars are not heroin."

"No, but they're contraband."

"Only in the United States. He smoked 'em all the time. Said tobacco had no politics."

Brubaker removed his own cigar and looked at it. "And I have to smoke these goddamned ropes." He shrugged. "Oh, well, if Castro was chairman of the Republican National Committee, I still couldn't afford his cigars."

"Well, look," Romstead said. "It seems to me there's a big hole in your reasoning somewhere. If he bought this crap for a quarter million dollars, as you say, and then sold it to somebody else at a profit, he must have got more than forty dollars for it. It wasn't at the house, and it wasn't in the apartment, so what happened to it?"

"Those hoods got it, obviously. The same time they got him."

17

"It must have been at the house, then, if they came up here looking for him. Was there any sign of a fight?"

"None at all. But don't forget, he was playing with professionals. They don't come on like Laurel and Hardy."

"You're convinced of that? Then there's not much chance of catching them?"

There was a sudden darkening of anger in the chief deputy's face, gone just as quickly as he got it under control. "Jesus Christ, Romstead, I know how you feel, but look at the hole *we're* in. It wasn't anybody here that killed your father. We're just a geographical accident; all we've got is a dead body and jurisdiction. Everything leading up to the crime and everybody connected with it came from a metropolitan area in another state.

"The police down there are cooperating with us all they can, but they're shorthanded and overworked the same as everybody else, and every detective on the force has got his own backlog of unsolved cases as long as a whore's dream. Our only chance is to keep questioning people, the same as we have been ever since it happened, till we locate somebody who saw that car that night, to get some kind of description of it, a place to start. Your father had an unlisted telephone number and a post office box address, so they had to ask somebody to find out where he lived."

Brubaker began to put the file back into the folder. There were several questions Romstead wanted to ask, but they could be answered by Bolling just as well or maybe better. "We'll let you know when we come up with anything," Brubaker concluded.

Romstead stood up, and they shook hands. "Thanks for your time."

"Not at all. Incidentally, who's the owner of that boat you were on?"

"A man named Carroll Brooks. You can reach him at the Southland Trust Bank in San Diego."

Brubaker shrugged. "Just standard routine."

"No sweat." Romstead went out and walked over to Aspen Street, trying to collect his thoughts. What in God's name had the old man intended to do with a quarter million dollars in cash, even assuming he had that much in the first place? Why'd he bought a farm here, or ranch, or whatever it was, and then rented an apartment in San Francisco? The whole thing seemed to get murkier by the minute.

Bolling's office was on the third floor of the Whittaker Building, a large corner room with windows on two sides. The desk was a massive one of some dark wood, the carpet was gray, and there were two leather armchairs. The walls were lined with identically bound volumes of an extensive law library. Bolling himself appeared to be well into his sixties, but erect, with a homely, angular face and sparse white hair. The eyes were a sharp and piercing blue. He smiled as he got up from behind the desk. "By God, you're almost as big as he was."

"Not quite," Romstead said.

"Somehow I expected you to be darker, since your mother was Cuban, but you look exactly like him."

"She was blond, too."

"He said you were quite a baseball player."

"Prep school and in college," Romstead replied.

"Professional, too, I understand."

"I only lasted one season; I couldn't hit big-league pitching. It was a way to get through school, but I couldn't see minor-league ball as a career."

"You put yourself through college?"

"Not entirely. I had a jock scholarship and worked sum-

19

mers, but he sent me money and would have sent more, but I didn't need it."

"You're in his will, of course. Or have you seen a copy of it?"

"No. I didn't even know he had one." Romstead paused and then went on musingly. "I guess the reason I've never thought about it is that I must've always assumed he'd outlive me. I know that sounds crazy as hell—"

"No. Not to anybody who knew him. You haven't seen his place, of course?"

"No. I didn't even know about it until last night. And now I've just found out he had an apartment in San Francisco."

Bolling nodded. "He rented it about five months ago. I tried to talk him out of it, but he insisted."

"But why?"

"Why did I advise against it, you mean? On account of taxes."

"No, I mean the whole bit. Why did he retire here, and buy a place, and then rent an apartment there?"

"There were several reasons, actually, but the primary one, of course, was taxes. It's easy to get to San Francisco, which he loved, but still not in California, which he detested. But the sad truth is he was bored here, and he spent more and more time in San Francisco, going over for the opera, concerts, plays, and so on, always having to get confirmed hotel reservations each time, so he decided to rent the apartment. He said that as long as his voting residence was here and he owned property here and only spent a total of a couple of months a year in San Francisco, California could go to hell for its income and inheritance taxes. He was a very stubborn man, and beyond a point there was no use arguing with him."

"But why this obsession with taxes? Would it have made that much difference?"

"Well, considerable. Your father's income was in excess of fifty thousand a year, from his retirement pay and his securities. A lot of it was political bias, however; he loathed the whole idea of the welfare state, Social Security, unemployment benefits, the welfare rolls, and so on. He was a very charming and talented man, but politically he was somewhere off to the right of the Hapsburgs and Plantagenets."

"And it's true, then? He was a millionaire?"

"Oh, yes. His net worth was considerably over a million."

"Well, you don't believe that crap of Brubaker's, do you, that he was mixed up in the drug racket?"

"No," Bolling said. "Of course not. He said he made it in the stock market, and I see no reason to doubt it." He reached into a drawer for a document bound in blue paper and set it before him. "I won't bother to read you all this at the moment because a good deal of it is meaningless now until somebody finds out what happened to that two hundred and fifty thousand dollars." He glanced up. "Brubaker told you about it?"

Romstead nodded. "But why do you think he drew it out in cash? And what did he do with it?"

"I couldn't even guess," Bolling replied. "I've been racking my brains for ten days, and I get absolutely nowhere. It was a stupid thing to do, and your father was far from a stupid man. But what we're concerned with right here is that there are two immediate effects regarding the will, and one of them, I'm sorry to say, is very bad news for you. If that money is never recovered, you bear the whole loss."

"How's that?" Romstead asked.

"All the other bequests were fixed sums, and you were to get the residue of the estate."

Romstead tried to think of something to say, but there didn't appear to be anything. There was a moment of silence, and then Bolling asked, "You understand what I'm saying?"

"Oh— Sure. I guess I was just savoring the moment. How many other people have lost a quarter million dollars in a few seconds?"

There was admiration in Bolling's smile and shake of the head. "Well, I'm glad you don't shatter easily."

"Oh, it's not all that heroic," Romstead protested. "You might say I didn't have it long enough to get attached to it."

"Our only hope is that it may be recovered yet."

"Could he have deposited it in another bank? Or stashed it in a safe-deposit box?"

"No. We've exhausted that possibility—with help from the police, of course. We've checked every bank chain in California and Nevada and even furnished a description just in case he used another name for some unknown reason. Not a trace."

"Doesn't look very promising," Romstead said. "But what was the other effect you referred to?"

"On probating the will and settling the estate. The whole thing's at a standstill, for the reason that we don't know how much the estate is."

"I see what you mean. For federal tax purposes?"

"Sure. It would make a big difference. And the tax people don't accept figures like give-or-take-a-quarter-million-dollars. As far as they're concerned, the last person to have possession of that money was your father, and if that wasn't the case, it's up to him—or us, that is—to prove otherwise. If he bought something with it, whatever he bought has to be appraised and the arrived-at value added to the tax-liable value of the estate. If it was stolen from him between the time he drew it out and the time he died, that might change the picture, but we'd have to prove it was stolen, and when, where, and by whom, and if we were in a position to do all that, we could probably recover it anyway.

"Practically all of your father's worth is in securities; the only real property he owned is his place here, which consists of ten acres, the dwelling and other structures, and furnishings. Total assessed value, about seventy-five thousand dollars. You inherit that, along with the car, plus whatever's left after taxes, bequests to the San Francisco Opera Association, the San Francisco Symphony, and three women in Europe and the Far East that I gather are old girlfriends. If the other money's never recovered, but is still taxed, that'll be roughly eighty thousand.

"So as it stands now, you'll get a a little over a hundred and fifty thousand dollars instead of the four hundred thousand dollars it would have been."

Romstead nodded. "Well, that's considerably better than a kick in the ass with a frozen boot. I didn't expect anything." He went on. "But about that money—how'd he draw it out? He surely didn't keep anything like that in a checking account?"

"Oh, no. He asked his broker to sell securities in that amount and deposit the proceeds in the bank."

"In person or over the phone?"

"On the phone."

"What day was this?"

"July sixth, I think—just a minute." Bolling pressed a lever and spoke into the intercom. "Rita, will you bring me that file on Captain Romstead?"

The gray-haired, rather matronly secretary came in with a file folder and went back out, closing the door. Bolling consulted some of the papers in it. "His brokers are a small firm, Winegaard and Stevens; it was Winegaard who handled his business. Your father called him just at seven A.M. on Thursday, July sixth—that's local time, of course, which would be the opening of the New York Stock Exchange. He read him a list of securities to sell and asked him to deposit the proceeds in his checking account at the Northern California First National Bank, which is practically next door on Montgomery Street. He said to sell it all at the market opening and to expedite the deal as much as he could; he needed the money not later than the following Wednesday, which would be the twelfth. The deposit would still have to clear, of course, before it could be drawn on."

"Then did he alert the bank?"

"Yes. On Monday, the tenth, he called and talked to Owen Richter, one of the officers he knew personally. Told him about the upcoming deposit, asked him to clear it as fast as he could, and told him he was going to want it in cash, so they'd be prepared."

"Did he ask Richter to call him when it cleared?"

"No. He said he'd call back himself. Which he did, Wednesday morning. The money was there, so he came in and picked it up."

"Was he alone?"

"Yes. I specifically asked Richter about that. He said there was nobody with him at all. He seemed to be perfectly all right, rational and sober. He got a little abrasive when Richter tried to talk him out of taking it in cash, and he didn't offer any further explanation except that it was for a business deal; but both of these are entirely characteristic of the captain in the best of circumstances. He seldom explained anything, and he had a very low tolerance for unsolicited advice."

Romstead nodded, puzzled. "And Winegaard didn't get any further explanation either?"

"No." Bolling smiled faintly. "I doubt he expected much; he'd dealt with your father a long time. The only thing he objected to was the selection of the stocks to sell."

"How was that?"

"Well, normally, of course, if you're liquidating part of a

portfolio for some reason, you do it selectively, that is, you prune out the weak sisters, the indifferent performers, losers where you want to cut your losses, and so on. He didn't do that. He just went straight down the list until the total added up to a little over two hundred and fifty thousand and told Winegaard to sell it all."

"That doesn't make sense."

"No. Certainly not for a man who'd managed to make a fortune in the stock market over the years. As I say, Winegaard objected, or tried to, but he was cut off pretty sharply."

"I don't get it." Romstead shook his head. "Oh, how about the burial expenses? Are there any accounts to settle?"

"No. They're all taken care of."

"Then you paid them, as executor of the estate?"

"No, he did. At the time he drew up his will, just shortly after he moved here, he made all the arrangements with the mortuary and paid for his own funeral in advance. Also the headstone."

"Why? You don't suppose he had some warning this was going to happen?"

"Oh, no, that wasn't it. It was just that he took a dim view of the whole overblown ritual and what he considered the funeral industry's exploitation of family grief. Said it'd do them good now and then to have to deal with a hardheaded businessman who was still alive. So he picked out the cheapest package they had, beat them down to the rock-bottom price, and paid it and gave me the receipt. I pointed out that since he'd probably live to a hundred and ten, he was losing the interest on the money, but he said with the chronic rate of inflation he wasn't losing a cent. And he was right, when you stop to think of it."

"Yeah. And then the same man's supposed to have gone wandering around the streets of San Francisco like some kind of nut with a suitcase full of money."

25

Bolling spread his hands. "The same man."

Romstead stood up. "Well, thanks for filling me in, Mr. Bolling. I won't take up any more of your time."

"We'll be in touch with you. Are you going back to San Francisco right away?"

"Tonight, probably, or early in the morning. I'd like to drive by and see the place, if you'll tell me how to find it."

"We'll lend you a key so you can get in." They went out into the anteroom, and Bolling took a tagged house key from a safe.

"Just be sure everything's locked when you leave. Go straight west here on Third Street. It's on the right, about four miles, a ranch-style house a hundred yards back from the road, white brick and redwood with a red tile roof."

He went back to the motel and got the car. He wanted to call Mayo, but it was too early yet.

III

HE checked the odometer as he made the turn into Third. After a few blocks of residential district and a close-in area of small farms and orchards, the two-lane blacktop ran unfenced through the sage with a low ridge to his right. There was very little traffic until a big Continental suddenly materialized in his rearview mirror as it overhauled him at high speed. It started to pass but braked and swung back, tailgating right under his bumper, as a pickup truck came toward them in the other lane.

The pickup went past; the Continental burst from behind him with a shriek of rubber and went on. He caught a brief glimpse of a blond woman behind the wheel as it flashed past. She was scarcely a hundred yards ahead of him when she abruptly hit the brakes again, forcing him to slow down to keep from running up on her as she swung off the road onto a driveway running up the hill between twin lines of white-painted fence. He muttered with annoyance. And they talked about California drivers killing themselves. There was a sprawling low-roofed ranch house at the top of the hill, and beside the road a white mailbox with the name Carmody. The mailbox was supported by a serpentine column of welded links of chain.

A few hundred yards ahead the road curved to the right around the end of the ridge, and he saw the place. There was a cattle guard through the fence and a red gravel drive leading back to the house, which was the only one in sight as the road swung left again and disappeared over a rise a quarter mile away. He turned in.

He stopped in front of the attached two-car garage at the right end of the house and got out. In the intense silence his shoes made a harsh grating sound on the gravel. There was a flagstone walk bordered by flower beds leading to the front door, and in front of that a considerable area of some kind of ground cover he thought was ivy. Beyond the far corner of the house was a large cottonwood. The big swing-up door of the garage was closed, and curtains were drawn over all the windows in front. The red gravel drive continued on past the side of the garage toward the rear. He walked back.

There was a wide expanse of flagstone terrace here, extending between the two wings of the house and outward toward the rear. Farther back were a redwood shed, which was probably the pump house for the well, and then a white-painted corral fence and a small barn. At the top of the sloping hillside to his right he could see some trees and part of a patio wall which must be the rear of the Carmody place.

He went back around in front and let himself in with the key Bolling had given him. There was a small vestibule just inside, floored with dark ceramic tile. The air was stale, as in a house closed and unoccupied for a long time, and underlaid with the ghosts of uncounted cigars. The back of the entryway opened into one end of the living room, while a door on the right led to the kitchen, which was along the front of the house. Another door on the left connected with a hallway along the bedroom wing.

He crossed the kitchen and opened the door at the far end of it. The garage had no windows, and the light was poor. He flicked a switch, doubtful that anything would happen, but two overhead lights came on. The pump, he thought; they'd had to leave the power on because of the water system and the automatic sprinklers. The car was a blue Mercedes. It bore a heavy coating of powdery white dust, and the windshield was smeared with spattered insects. It had been on a long trip at high speed, all right, but he frowned, wondering how it had got that dusty driving to San Francisco. Well, maybe it had been that way before the trip.

There was no doubt Brubaker had already done it, but he opened the left front door and checked the lubrication record stuck to the frame. "Jerry's Shell Service, Coleville, Nevada," it said, and the date of the last service was July 4, 1972. Oil change and lubrication at 13,037. He leaned in and read the odometer. It stood at 13,937. That was more than 800 miles. San Francisco was—call it 270, round trip 540. So the old man had driven another 300 miles somewhere in that time between July 4 and 14. Well, that could be anything—or nothing.

He switched off the lights and went back into the kitchen, pushing the button in the doorknob to relock the door. There was another entrance to the combined living room and dining room from this end of the kitchen. It was a long room with a deep shag carpet, and most of the opposite wall was covered by drawn white drapes. At the right were a dining table and then a teak buffet and a long sofa sitting back to back to divide it from the living-room area. In the latter there were two large armchairs and a coffee table and a white brick fireplace, but the first and overall impression was of books, record albums, and hi-fi equipment.

He started toward that end of the room, but as he passed the end of the sofa, he saw a piece of luggage sitting on it. There was a faintly jarring incongruity about it in this otherwise neat and well-ordered room, and he stopped, for some reason remembering his question to Brubaker on whether there had been any sign of a fight. Why would somebody with a seaman's passion for a-place-for-everything-and-everything-in-its-place leave his suitcase in the living room?

It was a small streamlined case of black fiber glass with no identification on it of any kind. He flipped the latches. It was unlocked. On top was a folded brown silk dressing gown. He lifted it out of the way and poked through the contents beneath it: pajamas, a rolled pair of socks, a laundered shirt in plastic, a couple of ties, a pair of shorts, and a plastic bag containing a soiled shirt and some more underwear. At the bottom were a zippered leather toilet kit, a half-empty box of Upmann cigars, and some books of paper matches variously advertising a San Francisco restaurant, a Las Vegas hotel, and a savings and loan association. He shrugged. There was nothing of interest here, and Brubaker had no doubt already searched it anyway.

But why was it here? He idly lifted one of the aluminum tubes from the cigar box, twisted off the cap, and slid the cigar out. It was encased in a thin curl of wood veneer and then a tightly rolled paper wrapper. He removed these and sniffed it. He'd smoked cigars for a brief period in his early twenties before he'd given up smoking altogether, but even after all these years he could still appreciate the aroma. He went out into the kitchen, found a knife in one of the drawers, cut the tip off it, and lighted it with one of the paper matches.

He took a deep, appraising puff, removed it from his mouth, let the smoke out slowly, and gestured with judicial approval. If you had to kill yourself, do it in the imperial manner; arrive at the operating room for the thoracotomy on a stretcher of royal purple borne by Nubian slaves. He picked up the silk robe to put it back in the bag; something slithered out of its folds, something golden and soft that might have been the pelt of some unfortunate honey-colored animal or the scalp of a Scandinavian settler. It was a hair-piece; a fall, he thought, was the correct terminology.

He looked at it helplessly for a moment and then sighed. That certainly didn't raise any doubts it was the old man's case; if you looked at it in the light of history, it merely confirmed it. No doubt his mother, unless she'd forsworn the practice early in the game, could have suited up an average sorority by filtering the old rooster's bags for lipsticks, mascara pencils, pants, bras, and earrings. While it sure as hell could help answer a great many questions if you knew the identity of this moulting San Francisco roommate and where she was now, at the moment it was of no help at all. He dropped the fall back in, folded the robe over it, and closed the bag. He wondered if Brubaker had spotted it and then decided he wouldn't be much of a cop if he hadn't.

Big hi-fi speakers were mounted in the corners of the living room opposite the sofa. They'd been housed in some dark wood he thought was ebony. The components—turntable, FM tuner, and amplifier—were mounted on teak shelves in the center of the same wall, themselves encased in the same wood as the speakers. Above and on both sides were shelves of operatic and symphonic albums, several hundred of them at a conservative guess. Most of the balance of the wall space was taken up with books. Romstead walked over and ran his eye along the rows, lost in admiration for the far-ranging and cultivated mind of a man whose formal education had ended at the age of fourteen. Though mostly in English, there were some in German and French and his native Norwegian, and they ranged from novels and biography to poetry and mathematics.

His thoughts broke off suddenly at the sound of a car coming up the drive, scattering gravel. He stepped out into the kitchen and parted the curtains above the sink just as it slid to a stop behind his and the driver got out and slammed the door. It was the hell-for-leather Valkyrie in the Continental.

She was five eight, at least, a statuesque figure of a woman clad in a peasant blouse and skirt in a flamboyant combination of colors and snugged in at their juncture around a surprisingly slender waist considering the amplitude of the bust above and rounded hips below. The tanned legs were bare, and her shoes appeared to consist principally of cork platforms an inch and a half thick. She carried an oversized straw handbag in the crook of her left arm and moved with a self-assured sexy swing as she came toward the flagstone walk. Romstead noted the shade of the rather carelessly swirled blond hair, and his eyes were coldly speculative as he let the curtain fall back in place. In a moment the doorbell chimed. He went out into the vestibule and opened the door. She looked up at him; the blue eyes went wide, and she gasped.

"Oh, no! Even the cigar!"

He removed it from his mouth. "I stole it," he said. "It belongs to the United States Customs."

"Well, that figures, too." She gave a flustered smile then that didn't quite match the eyes. "Excuse me, I don't know *what* I'm saying, you startled me so, the very *image* of him —I mean younger, naturally—but when you just *loomed* up there at me puffing on the same cigar—oh, heavens, I'm Paulette Carmody, your next-door neighbor."

"How do you do," he said. "Won't you come in?"

She preceded him into the living room and sat down on the sofa right beside the suitcase with no apparent notice of it while girlish chatter continued to pour forth like whipped cream from a ruptured aerosol can.

"—just now heard you were in town, and then it struck me, I mean, that car I'd passed on the road, it *did* have California tags, and I was just positive I'd seen San Francisco on the dealer's license plate holder, and I said I'll bet *any-thing* that was Eric—"

She had crossed her legs, revealing an interesting expanse of golden thigh, and Romstead reflected that if the front of that peasant blouse were cut any lower, she'd better never lean down or frothy conversation wouldn't be the only thing to well forth. He wondered about it. Maybe she was a harmless fluffbrain, but he didn't think so. She was forty to forty-five, and she'd been around. There were intelligence and tough-mindedness in there somewhere. He listened with grave courtesy while she said what an *awful* thing it had been and she wanted him to know how sorry she was.

"Are you moving in?" she asked then.

"Oh, no," he replied. "I just borrowed a key to have a look."

"Oh, I see." She gestured. "I thought perhaps the suitcase was yours."

"No." He shrugged. "I just assumed it was his. It was sitting there when I came in." Ma'am, there's nobody here but us chickens, and you know we wouldn't have searched it. "I wish I could offer you a drink or something."

"You know, I could use a beer. He always kept some Tuborg in the refrigerator."

"I'll see." He went out into the kitchen. There were several bottles of beer. He listened intently for the sound of the latches, but her continued chatter would have covered it if there were any. Somehow he'd have to get a peek into that straw handbag. He found some glasses and a bottle opener and poured the beer. He went back, and on the opposite side of the case from her there was just a fraction of an inch of brown silk showing where she hadn't got all the robe back in. He handed her the glass and sat down.

"Thank you, Eric." She smiled. "As I was saying, he was the most fascinating man I ever met—"

"You'd better run it through a laundromat before you wear it again," he said.

"What?" Just for a second the confusion showed. "I don't understand—. Wear what?"

"The doily. It's been shut up in a suitcase for two weeks with a box of cigars. It'll smell like the end of a four-day poker game."

"Well!" The outrage was just about to become airborne when it collapsed in a gurgle of amusement that gave way to laughter. "Oh, crap! So you had found it." She lifted the hairpiece from her handbag, sniffed it, made a face, and dropped it back.

"It was a stupid thing to try, anyway," he said. "Brubaker's bound to have seen it when he searched the house, and he'll know you were the only one who had a chance to get it back."

She shrugged, took a pack of filter cigarettes from the handbag, and lighted one. "Brubaker could already make a damned good guess whose it is, but he's not about to."

"Why not?"

"He'd have to be ready to prove it, for one thing, unless he likes the odor of singed tail feathers. Also, he'd have to be damned sure it had anything to do with what happened to your father. Which it didn't."

"That remains to be seen. But he could sure as hell sweat some answers out of you about what the old man was doing in San Francisco and why he needed that money."

She shook her head. "I wasn't in San Francisco with him."

"Sure. You just loaned him the rug. He was going to audition for a job at Finocchio's—"

"Oh, I was with him, all right, but it was in Las Vegas."

"What? I mean—when?"

"Before he went to San Francisco. We drove down on the Fourth—"

34

"Hold it. You say you drove? Which car?"

"His."

"How far is it?"

"Four hundred and five miles. We checked it."

"Excuse me a minute." He strode out to the garage and opened the door of the Mercedes to check the figures again: 13,937 less 13,073 was—864. Twice 405 was 810. That left only 54 miles unaccounted for.

"What is it?" She had come out and was standing in the kitchen doorway.

He indicated the service sticker. "He couldn't have driven the car to San Francisco. Or even to Reno to take a plane." He repeated the figures. "So how did he get there?"

"Maybe somebody else drove him to the airport."

"You'd think whoever it was would have said so by this time. Anyway, Brubaker checked the airlines; he had no reservation any time in that period."

She frowned. "Well, we'd better tell him. I didn't know about this mileage bit."

"I'll do it. Maybe he won't lean on me for the name."

"Oh, hell, that's all right. I mean, if it's important to the investigation. I'm not married, now. Or running for the school board."

"Was the car this dusty when you got back?" he asked.

"I don't know," she said. "It was dark. But I don't see why it would have been; we certainly didn't drive on any country roads, going or coming, and it wasn't dusty like that when we got there."

He nodded. Then a good part of that 54 miles had been on a dirt road. They went back to the living room, and he retrieved his beer. "How long did you stay in Las Vegas?" he asked.

"That night and the next day. I think we started back around eleven P.M. Anyway, he let me off at my place just

35

a few minutes before five A.M." She sighed. "Forty hours with about two hours' sleep. God, I'm glad I didn't have to try to keep up with him when he was twenty-eight—"

"Wait a minute," Romstead interrupted. "That'd have to be five A.M., the sixth?"

"Hmmmm—yes, that's right."

Just two hours, he thought, before he'd called Winegaard with that sell order. "Well, look, did he go in the bucket in Las Vegas? I mean, on the cuff, for really big money?"

She smiled. "God, no. I doubt he lost twenty dollars. Gambling—or that kind of gambling—bored him to death. He said anybody with any respect for mathematics would have to be insane to think he could beat a house percentage and a limit. He just liked the shows, and the fact that nobody ever goes to bed—to sleep, anyway."

"Well, did he tell you he was going to San Francisco?"

"No."

"That's funny. No mention of it at all?"

"Not a word. If it'd been anybody else, it would have puzzled hell out of me. I mean, if he was planning to take off again just as soon as we got home, you'd think he'd have said something about it, just to make conversation if nothing else, but that's the way he operated."

"But nobody knows for sure when he did leave."

"Oh, it was within a few hours. Don't ask me how in hell he could do it, but he was gone again before noon."

"How do you know?"

"That's when I woke up. When I started to unpack my bags, I noticed the fall was missing, so I called to see if I'd put it in his by mistake. No answer. I tried again several times in the afternoon and gave up."

"Well, did he say anything about a business deal?"

"Absolutely nothing. But then he wouldn't have; he never did."

"You know Brubaker's theory? That he was mixed up in the drug traffic."

"Bullshit."

"I'm glad you don't believe it. But I guess we're in the minority."

"Darling, I have no illusions at all about your old man; I've known him longer than you think I have. He was arrogant, pigheaded, and intolerant, he had the sex drive and the fidelity of a stallion, and any woman who could stay married to him for fifteen years the way your mother did could qualify for instant sainthood; but he wasn't a criminal."

"You knew him before he moved here?"

"*Umh-umh.* He saved my life, a few years back."

"How's that?"

"It sounds a little kooky, out here in the sagebrush, but would you believe a rescue at sea?" She glanced at her watch and stood up. "But I've got to run. If you'll stop by when you get through here, I'll hammer together a couple of bloody Marys and a bite of lunch and tell you about it."

"I'd love to. Thank you."

He went out with her and down the walk. As she started to get into the Continental, there was a sudden wild clatter of the pipes in the cattle guard beyond them, and a dusty green Porsche came snarling up the drive. It pulled off and stopped on the other side of her. When the driver emerged and slammed the door, there was more an impression he had simply removed the car like an article of clothing and tossed it aside rather than got out of it, and Romstead thought of the old joke about one of the Rams' linemen: When he couldn't find a place to park his VW, he just carried it around with him.

While he wasn't quite that big, he would have made an ominous hunk of linebacker staring hungrily across the big butts at a quarterback. He was pushing forty now, Romstead

37

thought, and a little gone to belly, but not too much, and the pale eyes were mean as he padded around the rear of the Continental. Something was riding him.

"I tried to call you," he said to Paulette Carmody. "Carmelita said you were down here. Figures."

"Lew," she began the introduction, "this is Eric—"

He cut her off. "I know who he is." The eyes flicked contemptuously across Romstead and dismissed him along with the rest of the scenery. "Have you seen Jeri?"

"*Mr. Bonner.*" The tone was sweetly dangerous. "May I present—" She broke off herself then. "Jeri? You mean she's here in town?"

"She came in last Tuesday. But when I woke up awhile ago, she was gone. No note or anything."

"I'll see you up at the house," Paulette said.

"Right." Before he turned away, Bonner swept Romstead with that flat stare again. "Going to take over the family business?"

"Shut up, Lew!" Paulette snapped. Romstead stared thoughtfully after him but said nothing. The Porsche shot back down the drive.

"I'm sorry," Paulette said. "Usually he has at least as much social grace as a goat, but he's a little off his form today."

Romstead shrugged. "Something's chewing on him."

"It's his sister. I'm worried about her, too."

"Who is he?"

"He used to work for my husband, and before that, he played pro football, one of the Canadian teams. Owns a liquor store now." She got into the car. "See you in a little while."

"Hadn't I better skip it?" He nodded after the Porsche now disappearing around the bend in the highway. "I don't think we're going to grow on each other, and it'll just be unpleasant for you."

38

"Oh, he'll be gone before then."

She swung the big car and went back down the drive. Romstead returned to the house. He rinsed out the two glasses and dropped the beer bottles in the kitchen garbage can. There was another room in this wing of the house, directly back of the garage, its entrance through a doorway at the rear of the dining area. He went in.

It was a library or den. There was another fireplace, a big easy chair with a reading lamp, a desk, and a coffee table. On the walls were more books, an aneroid barometer, some carved African masks, a bolo, a pair of spears, and several abstract paintings. A magazine rack held copies of *Fortune*, *Time*, and *Scientific American*. The cigars were in a closet, each box individually wrapped and sealed in plastic.

In the other wing the small bedroom at the front of the house was apparently a guest room. The next door down the hall was a bathroom. He glanced in briefly and went on. The master bedroom was at the rear. He stepped in and stopped abruptly in surprise. After the neatness of the rest of the house it was a mess.

It was a big room containing a king-sized double bed with a black headboard and matching night tables with big lamps on each side. One of the lamps was lighted. The drapes, the same dark green as the bedspread, were all closed. Off to his left, the door to the bathroom was ajar, and he could see a light was on in there too. Beyond the bathroom door was a large dresser, all its drawers pulled open and their contents—shirts, socks, underwear, handkerchiefs, boxes of cuff links, pajamas—thrown out on the rug.

On top of it was a woman's handbag, open and lying on its side, a kitchen knife, a spoon, a hypodermic syringe, and a small plastic bag containing some fraction of an ounce of a white powder. He strode on in to look at the floor on the other side of the bed. A yellow dress and a pair of scuffed

39

and dusty pumps with grotesque square heels lay on the rug beside it. Next to them on a hassock were a slip, nylon pants, and a bra. There was no sound at all from the bathroom. He felt the hair prickle on the back of his neck as he went over and slowly pushed the door open.

To his left was a stall shower and at the other end the commode and washbasin. The oversized tub was directly opposite, a slender leg draped over the side of it with the doubled knee of the other leg visible just beyond. He stepped on in and looked down. She was lying on her back, her head under the spigot and turned slightly to one side with the long dark-red hair plastered across her face so that little of it was visible except the chin and part of the mouth. There was about an inch of water in the bottom of the tub, but no blood and no marks of violence on her body.

The tub had apparently been full when she fell in, but owing to an imperfectly fitting plug in the mechanical drain assembly, the water had slowly leaked out over the hours, leaving her hair to settle like seaweed across her face. There was no need to touch her to verify it; she'd been dead from the time she fell in. Had she struck her head on the spigot? There was no hair stuck to it, no blood. The heroin, he thought, or whatever that stuff was she'd shot herself with. But, hell, even somebody drugged should be able to climb out of a bathtub before he drowned. He was suddenly conscious of the passage of time and that he was wasting it in disjointed and futile speculation when he'd better be calling the police. He whirled and went out.

IV

THERE was a telephone on one of the night tables. He grabbed it up, but it was dead; it had been disconnected. It was then he noticed the shards of broken glass on the rug against the far wall. He went over and parted the drapes above it. It was a casement window. She'd knocked out enough glass and then cut away part of the screen, probably with the kitchen knife, so she could reach in and unlatch it and crank it open. There was a wooden box on the ground beneath it, along with the remains of the screen. It was at the side of the house, so he hadn't seen it when he was out back.

But why in the name of God had she broken in here to shoot herself with that junk? He looked then at the scattered contents of the dresser drawers, at the mute evidence of her frenzy, and felt a little chill between his shoulder blades. But, damn it, Brubaker had searched the house. For Christ's sake, get going, he told himself. He ran out to the car.

He was out on the highway before he remembered he hadn't even closed the front door of the house. Well, it didn't matter. He made a skidding turn off the road and shot up the driveway toward the Carmody house, wondering now what the urgency was, since the woman was dead and had been since last night or maybe even the night before. Bonner's Porsche was parked in the circular blacktop drive under the big trees in front. He pulled up behind it and hurried up the walk to punch the bell. He heard it chime inside, and in a moment the door was opened by a pleasant dark-haired woman with liquid brown eyes.

"Could I use your phone?" he asked.

"I'll ask," she said. "What is your name?"

"Romstead." At that moment Paulette appeared in the small entry behind her. "Why, Eric, come on in."

He stepped inside. "I've got to use your phone. Something's happened."

Paulette smiled at the maid. "It's all right, Carmelita, I'll take care of it." Carmelita disappeared. Paulette led him through a doorway at the left into a long living room with a picture window and French doors at the back of it opening onto a flagstone deck and a pool. Bonner was sitting at a table under a big umbrella. He saw them and got up.

The phone was on a small desk across the room. He grabbed the directory, looked inside the cover for the emergency numbers, and dialed.

"What is it?" Paulette asked. "What happened?"

"There's a woman in the house. Dead."

"Oh, my God! Where?"

"Back bedroom. In the tub, drowned—"

"Sheriff's department. Orde," a voice answered.

"Could I speak to Brubaker?"

"Just a minute." There were a couple of clicks.

"Brubaker."

"This is Eric Romstead," he said. "I'm calling from Mrs. Carmody's. I've just come from my father's place, and there's a dead woman in the bath—"

His arm was grabbed by a big paw, and he was whirled around. It was Bonner, his face savage. "How old is she? What did she look like?"

Romstead jerked his arm away. "I don't know how old she is." He got the instrument back to his ear to hear the chief

42

deputy bark, "—the hell is going on there? Dead woman in whose bathroom—?"

"Captain Romstead's. She broke in a window."

"We'll be there in five minutes. Stay out of the house!"

He dropped the phone back on the cradle. Bonner lashed out at him, "God damn you, what did she look like?"

"I don't know," Romstead said. "Except she had red hair."

The big man wheeled and ran for the doorway. "Brubaker said to stay out," Romstead called, but he was gone. The front door slammed. Before he and Paulette could reach the walk outside, there was a snarl from the Porsche's engine and a shriek of rubber, and he was tearing down the drive. They got into Romstead's car and ran down the hill onto the highway. By the time they'd turned in through the cattle guard the Porsche had already come to a stop, and Bonner was running in the front door. He stopped behind the other car, but they did not get out. When he looked around at her, there were tears in her eyes.

"Maybe it's not," he said.

"Yes," she said. "She was one of the most beautiful girls I ever saw, and she had dark red hair."

"Was she on drugs? There was a needle in there."

"He was afraid she was."

"Where did she live?"

"San Francisco."

"She knew the old man?"

"Yes. How well, I don't know, but she was with my husband and me on that sailboat when he picked us up at sea. Could you tell what happened to her? Did she fall in the tub and knock herself out, or what?"

"I don't know," he said. "But my guess would be an overdose." He told her about the packet of heroin, or whatever it was, and the way the dresser had been ransacked.

"I don't get it," she said, baffled. "I just don't believe it—"

She broke off then as Bonner emerged from the house and walked slowly toward his car. They got out, but there was no need to ask.

"I'm so sorry, Lew," Paulette said.

He made no reply. He leaned his arms on top of the Porsche and stood, head lowered, staring at the ground. It wouldn't do any good, Romstead thought, and he might be just asking for it, but he had to say something.

"I'm sorry, Bonner," he said. "I'm sorry as hell about it."

Bonner spoke without looking around, his voice little more than a ragged whisper. "Don't bump me," he said. "Don't crowd me at all."

It was hot in the room, and there was a strained, tense silence as they waited for Brubaker and the others to finish in the bedroom. Romstead had drawn the drapes and opened the sliding glass door to get a movement of air through it, but it didn't help much. Bonner stood with his back to the others, looking out at the terrace. Paulette Carmody was smoking a third cigarette. Romstead stared at the rows of books without seeing them. The coroner had gone now, as well as a deputy with a camera, the picture taking completed. Two men came out through the vestibule carrying the sheeted figure on a stretcher. Brubaker was behind them. He watched the body go out to the waiting ambulance, his face bitter.

"Junk," he said. "Goddamned junk."

Bonner spoke without turning. "Nice she knew where to find it."

Romstead said nothing. What could he say? He asked himself. There was no use trying to kid himself or anybody else the girl had had the stuff with her. She hadn't walked four miles in the dark and illegally broken into a house to take a bath. There was no use even conjecturing on how it had got here, but there it was. The girl was dead because of it, and Bonner was running very near the edge, so this might be one of the really great opportunities of a lifetime to keep his mouth shut.

"It looks like just another overdose," Brubaker said. "There are no marks on her of any kind, she didn't fall and hit her head, and there's no evidence anybody else was in the room. We're checking for prints as a matter of routine, but we're pretty sure what happened is that it was pure heroin instead of being cut four or five to one, and she took too much. The autopsy and lab tests should verify it."

"But," Paulette interrupted, "why was she in the tub?"

"Don't forget she'd just walked four miles, probably running half the time, and she was suffering withdrawal symptoms—a couple of which are profuse sweating and screaming nerves. And she'd just walked into an addict's paradise—at least a week's supply of junk and a place nobody could find her and take it away from her. All she wanted was to get some of it into a vein, relax in a hot tub while her nerves uncoiled, and then float off for days. So just about the time she got the tub filled it hit her. She was probably sitting on the side of it testing the water, and she went over backward into it. She drowned, technically, but she'd have been dead anyway."

"If you want to ask me any questions," Bonner said harshly, "ask 'em. I'd like to get out of this place."

"You say she came back last week? How?"

"On the bus. She said she'd quit her job and wanted to stay a few weeks while she made up her mind what to do. But she worried me, the way she acted."

"How?"

"She couldn't seem to decide on anything. One minute she was going to New York; then it was Los Angeles, and then Miami. She was going to try modeling; then she was

45

going to study computer programming. I told her I'd lend her the money for any kind of trade school she wanted or even for college if she wanted to go back. She'd be all for it, and half an hour later it was out; she was going to get a job on a cruise ship or hook up with some couple sailing around the world. The only thing she never mentioned was going back to San Francisco, which was screwy, because she was always crazy about it."

Brubaker frowned. "Well, did she see any of her friends?"

"No. She didn't even want anybody to know she was here. She was nervous as a cat, pacing all the time, but she wouldn't budge out of the house. I told her she could use the car any time she wanted it and asked her why she didn't drive out to Paulette's and visit and have a swim, but no, she didn't want to see anybody. She'd jump six feet when the phone rang, or the doorbell—"

"And you didn't know she was on the stuff? There were needle tracks all over her arm."

"God damn it, maybe I didn't want to know! Anyway, she always wore things with sleeves like so—" Bonner made a slashing gesture with one hand across the other forearm.

"Three-quarters," Paulette said.

"When was the last time you saw her?" Brubaker asked.

"About two o'clock this morning."

"When you got home from the store?"

"Yeah. Her bedroom door was closed; but I looked in, and she was asleep."

Brubaker shook his head. "Probably faking it so you'd cork off and she could slip out. If she was desperate enough for a fix to walk four miles and burglarize a house, she wasn't sleeping, believe me."

"Well, why did she wait till I got home? I was at the store from six P.M. on, and she could have taken off any time."

"Maybe it still wasn't unbearable then, and she was trying

to sweat it out. She probably had a little she'd brought from San Francisco. Also, after two A.M. there'd be no traffic on the road and she wouldn't be seen. Did she ever mention Captain Romstead?"

"No, not that I recall."

"But she did know he was dead?"

"Yes. At least, I told her, but you could never be sure she was paying any attention to what you were saying. It didn't seem to interest her."

"Do you know whether she'd ever been in the house here?" Bonner's face was savage. "What do you mean by that?"

"Well, obviously she knew the stuff was in here and right where to find it."

It was Paulette who answered. "No, I don't think she was ever in here. As far as I can recall, a few days last Christmas was the only time she's been home since Captain Romstead moved here, and he was in San Francisco then."

Brubaker nodded, his face thoughtful. "That still leaves the question, then, of how she was so sure she'd find it here. . . . But I guess that's all, Lew, except I'm sorry as hell about it."

Bonner started out. He turned in the doorway and asked Paulette, "You want a lift home?"

"No, thanks, Lew. There's something else I want to see Mr. Brubaker about." She got up, however, and went out with him.

"How old was she?" Romstead asked.

"Twenty-four or twenty-five. Jesus Christ, that's what tears you up." Brubaker took a cigar from his pocket and started removing cellophane. They heard the Porsche go down the drive, and Paulette came back in.

"Good God, not that smudge pot," she said to Brubaker, "unless you want us to yell police brutality. Here." She flipped up the top of the black case, dug in it for the box of cigars, and held it out. He took it, completely deadpan, lifted out one of the tubes, and pulled the cap off, watching as she started to close the case again. Innocence itself, she flipped the robe out full length, folded it carefully, and replaced it so she could bring the lid down. He sighed.

"All right," he said. "Let's hear it."

She told him about the trip to Las Vegas. He went out to the garage to verify the mileage on the Mercedes. When he came back, he looked thoughtful, but he shook his head.

"So he just went to San Francisco with somebody else," he said. "Probably one of the outfit he was dealing with."

"But where did he go on that dirt road?" Romstead asked. "And why? If we could find the place—"

"You got any idea how many old ruts there are out there through the sagebrush and alkali flats in a radius of twenty-seven miles? To windmills and feeding stations and old mining claims? And if you did find it, I think what you'd see would be the wheel tracks and tail-skid marks of a light-plane."

"Why?"

"A lot of junk comes in from Mexico that way. And it could be how your father got to San Francisco."

Romstead tried once more, with the feeling he was only butting his head against a wall. "Look—he got back here at five A.M., and two hours later he was on the phone to his broker to raise two hundred and fifty thousand dollars in cash. There hadn't been a word about going to San Francisco or about a business deal. I think something happened in those two hours we don't know about."

"Sure. Because he hadn't said anything," Brubaker said wearily. "You ever hear of anybody on his way to pick up a shipment of junk that bought time on TV or took out an ad in the paper? Anyway, what is there to argue about now? I'd say Jeri Bonner had settled it once and for all."

It would always come down to that, Romstead thought, and it was unanswerable. Brubaker went on, "I'll admit I goofed to some extent; I searched the house, and I didn't see it; but I was looking for something the size of that suitcase, not a teabag."

"Incidentally," Romstead asked, "where was the suitcase? Did you find it right here?"

"No. It was in the trunk of the car. We brought it inside. They must have been waiting for him when he drove in."

"Since you keep begging me for my opinion—" Paulette said.

"All right. Go ahead."

"Your whole theory's horseshit. I don't have the faintest idea who killed Captain Romstead, or why, but he wasn't a drug peddler. And if Jeri found that heroin in this house, I say he didn't know it was here."

"Why?" Romstead asked. He had brought Paulette home, and they sat in the air-conditioned living room of her house with the bloody Marys she had promised. It was too hot now to sit out by the pool, and neither was interested in lunch with the death of Jeri Bonner weighing on their spirits. The Romstead house was locked up again, and Brubaker had said he would notify Sam Bolling so the broken window could be replaced. Romstead had given him the key to return. "I don't think he knew the stuff was there either," he went on, "but what makes you so sure of it?"

"Because I knew him. Better than anybody here." She set her drink on the coffee table between them and lit a cigarette. "I've heard his views on the subject, and like all the rest of his views, they were pretty strong. He had nothing but contempt for people who used drugs of any kind—except, of course, for *his* drugs: Havana cigars, brandy, and vintage champagne—and an even worse loathing for pushers and

smugglers who dealt in any of it, even marijuana. On the
Fairisle, his last command, he arrested one of his own crew
for trying to smuggle some heroin in on it. I mean, right
out of the eighteenth century, locked him up like Bligh
throwing somebody in the brig, and turned him over to the
federal agents when they docked. High-handed, oh, brother
—he could have been fired for it or picketed by every mari-
time union in the country, except that the man was guilty,
he had the heroin to prove it, and the guy was convicted
and sent to prison. That's no wild sea yarn, either; I knew
the nut myself. He was out in orbit, a dingaling with a hundred and sixty IQ. But I was going to tell you how we met,
almost five years ago."

She hesitated a moment, rattling the ice in her drink; then
she looked up with bubbling amusement. "This is a kooky
experience—I mean, telling a son about your affair with his
father. I feel like a dirty old woman or as if I were contribut-
ing to the delinquency of a minor."

"It's all right," Romstead said. "I'm precocious for thirty-
six."

"Good. I felt fairly certain you might be. . . . Anyway,
this happened in 1967. Steve—my husband—was a businessman, mostly real estate and land development, here in
Nevada and in Southern California; but his health was beginning to give him trouble, and he was semiretired. We lived
about half the time at our place in La Jolla and did quite
a bit of sailing. Steve had been an ocean-racing nut since
he was a young man, but he'd given that up when his health
began to fail. He sold the Ericson thirty-nine and bought
a thirty-six-foot cruising sloop a couple could handle, and
we planned to sail it to Honolulu, just the two of us.

"Then Lew Bonner asked us if we'd take Jeri. Lew was
working for Steve then, running a lumberyard and building
supply here in Coleville, and we both knew Jeri, of course,

and liked her. She was a real sweet kid, but becoming something of a hippie, and it bothered Lew a little. Most jocks are as square as Smokey the Bear, anyway—oops. The good old Carmody tact, but then I don't think of you as a jock, somehow."

Romstead shrugged. "Neither did the National League."

"Their parents were dead, and Lew had looked after her since she was sixteen. She'd been going to school at San Diego State but dropped out and was hanging out with a bunch of kids in Del Mar. She liked sailing and thought the trip would be groovy, or whatever the word was in 1967, so she came along.

"Everything went along fine until about a thousand miles out of Honolulu when we ran into a real bitch of a dustup. I don't think it ever reached gale force, actually, but it kept freshening while we were running before it, and before we knew it, we were carrying too much sail and had already carried it too damned long. We broached to, got knocked down, lost the mast and sails overboard, and shipped enough water to soak everything below. But the worst of it was Steve. He was badly hurt. He'd got thrown across the deck and landed on something that caught him just below the rib cage. He was in awful pain and could hardly move. The radio was drowned, so we couldn't call for help, and Jeri and I alone couldn't cope with that mess over the side. We made Steve as comfortable as we could with the painkillers from the medicine chest, but we were absolutely helpless.

"We were near the Los Angeles-Honolulu steamer lane, and late that afternoon we sighted a ship on the horizon and fired off some distress flares, but either it didn't see us or didn't give a damn, because it went on. And just about sunset, Steve died. I still wake up with a cold sweat, dreaming about that night. Jeri and I didn't think we'd ever see dawn

51

again, and before the night was over, we were so beaten we didn't really care a great deal whether we did or not. But when daylight did come there was another ship in sight, way off on the horizon. All we could do was fire off the last of our flares and pray. Then we saw it had changed course and was coming. It was the *Fairisle*.

"Your father sent over a boat and took us off. An autopsy was performed on Steve when we reached Honolulu, and the doctors said he'd died of internal bleeding from a ruptured spleen. I'd had it with oceans for all time, or thought I had. After I got back home and began to recover a little, I wrote the usual letters thanking him and the boat crew and also to the line praising him for his seamanship and for the royal way we'd been treated after we were picked up.

"That would have been the end of it, normally, except that about a year later I was in San Francisco on a shopping jag and walked out of the City of Paris one afternoon and bumped right into him. He invited me to have a drink. I don't know what *he* did three days later, when the tugs pulled the *Fairisle* away from the pier and she started down the bay, but I went back to the Mark and collapsed; I think I slept the clock around twice. Your father was one hell of a charming and fascinating man, and he had a way with women, as perhaps you've heard.

"When he came back from that trip, I was waiting for him in San Francisco, flew to Los Angeles to see him there, and then flew to Honolulu. The following trip I sailed with him, to Hong Kong, Kobe, and Manila—the *Fairisle* has accommodations for twelve passengers, you know. In the next three years I made three more trips to the Orient with him, and when he retired, I was partly responsible for his settling here. He wouldn't even consider La Jolla.

"There was never any question of marriage. I was in no hurry to be married again, and certainly not to him, and he

52

said from the start he'd never try it again, that he wasn't cut out for domesticity—which I could see even then was probably the understatement of the century.

"I have no doubt he had another girl, or perhaps several of them at different times, in San Francisco, but whether she or one of them was Jeri Bonner, I don't think so. She was only twenty-four, for one thing, and surprisingly, he didn't go for very young women. I know this is contrary to the classic pattern of the aging stud, needing younger and younger girls to get it off the runway, but maybe he was saving that phase for his eighties and nineties; his theory was that no woman under thirty even knew what it was all about. And there was the drugs; if she was using heroin, he wouldn't have had anything to do with her at all."

And still the stuff had been in the house, and she'd known it was and just where to find it, Romstead thought. You never came up with any answers, only more questions. And though he liked her, the sexy Mrs. Carmody's hymn to his father's virtuosity as a lover was beginning to bug him; he'd been twenty days at sea. He thanked her for the drink, went back to the motel, and called Mayo.

"What did you find out?" she asked.

"Nothing you'd believe," he said. "I'll tell you all about it when I get there. Around eleven P.M."

"I'll wait for you at your place."

"Good thinking."

"Sure. I thought it would be convenient. So if you're going to whizz through town in five minutes again, you can tell me about it while you're taking a cold shower."

"Let's make that ten instead of eleven."

He went out to the office, paid the toll charges, and left a call for five P.M. It was still a few minutes to ten that night when he emerged from the elevator in the high-rise complex

53

overlooking the Embarcadero and the bay and padded quietly along the carpeted hallway to his apartment.

The lights were dim in the living room. Mayo Foley, clad in a housecoat with apparently nothing under it, was listening to Ravel with her feet and long bare legs up on the coffee table beside a champagne bucket. She smiled, with that smoky look in the deep blue eyes he'd come to know so well, and said, "You're just in time, Romstead; I was about to start without you."

V

MAYO, whose real first name was Martha, was thirty-three, divorced, a creamy-skinned brunette with eyes that were very near to violet, and a registered nurse who'd always wanted to be a doctor but hadn't quite been able to make it into medical school after four years of premed at Berkeley. In spite of the med-school turndowns, she was only mildly hung up on women's lib, but she was a dedicated McGovernite and a passionate advocate of civil rights and environmental causes. She was also sexy as hell and possessed of a vocabulary that could raise welts on a Galápagos tortoise, as Romstead had learned early in their acquaintance when he'd jokingly called her a knee-jerk liberal. So far he had asked her at least three times to marry him, but she had refused, always gently, but decisively. Her first marriage had been a disaster, and she had reservations about him as a candidate for a second attempt.

He turned now and looked at her. She lay on her back, nude beside him in the faint illumination of the bedroom, totally relaxed, fluid, and pliant, a composition in chiaroscuro with the soft gleam of the thighs and the triangular wedge of velvet black at their juncture, the dark nipples of the spread and flattened breasts, pale blur of face, and the dark hair and the shadows of her eyes. This began to excite him again, and he turned and kissed her softly on the throat. It was after two in the morning now, and they had made love three times already, the last time very slowly and lingeringly, during which she had had a whole series of convulsive orgasms. Well, you could always try.

She pushed his hand away. "You've got a hell of a nerve, calling your father a stud."

"Cut it out. I haven't slept with another woman since I met you."

"Well, I should hope not. I don't see how you could work one into your schedule."

"It's just that I've been three weeks at sea. And I'm crazy about you."

She reached over on the nightstand and lighted a cigarette. The tip glowed red in the darkness. "What are you going to do?" she asked.

"Wait a few minutes and try again."

"Oh, *that* I know. If there'd been even the faintest doubt you'd keep trying, I'd have engulfed you like a Venus flytrap. You poor innocent, growing up in military schools." She puffed on the cigarette. Her nipples looked purple in the glow. "I mean, what are you going to do about your father and the money he left you?"

"Three things," he replied. "I thought about it all the way driving down tonight. I'll tell you the third one first, since it involves you. Instead of selling them, for a change I'm going to buy a boat. I mean, one whole hell of a lot of boat. Money will be no problem. I get about a hundred and fifty thousand from the estate, and I've got a little over that myself, savings and so on and the money I got for my franchise in Costa Rica—"

"You mean from the CIA."

"Are you still on that? I tell you I was working for myself."

"All right, all right, you were just an innocent businessman. Go on about the boat."

"Say a thirty-five to forty-foot ketch, which is about all two people can handle without having to work too hard

56

at it. Everything on it—self-steering vane, radiotelephone, fathometer, Kenyon log, diesel auxiliary, tanks for a cruising range of four hundred miles under power, generator, refrigerator. You can do all that with a fairly small boat if you're just putting in cruising accommodations for two, and you can do it for sixty thousand or less.

"We'll take a long cruise, down the west coast as far as Panama, across to the Galápagos, back up to Hawaii, and then out through the Marianas and Carolines. How about it?"

"Mmmmm—I don't know. I'll have to think about it."

"Why?"

"Let's don't go into that now. What are the other two things you're going to do?"

"The first is I'm going to find that son of a bitch who murdered the old man. And then I'm going to light one of those Havana cigars and smoke it very slowly right down to the end while he's begging me to call the police."

"And you wonder why I'm doubtful about marrying you."

"What does that mean?"

"You're just as arrogant and self-sufficient and ruthless as he was. Make up your own laws, and the hell with civilization."

"You ever hear of a place called Murmansk?" he asked.

"Sure. It's a Russian seaport in the Arctic. Why?"

He tried to tell her—dispassionately, of course, since this was hardly the setting for the kind of cold rage that had kept growing in him driving down from Nevada—tried to tell her of the gales, the snow, sleet, ships solidly encased in ice, dive-bomber attacks, submarine wolf packs, and the eternal, pitiless cold that could kill a man in the water in minutes. He hadn't known any of this at the time, of course; he was only a very young boy leading a very easy existence in an upper-class Havana suburb, but he'd learned it later

57

through reading about those convoy runs in World War II and what it was like to carry aviation gasoline and high explosives up across the top of the world while the Germans and the merciless Barents Sea did their level best to kill you. His father had done it, for months on end, along with a lot of other men who could have found cozier backwaters to ride out the war if they'd tried.

"He was out there taking his chances where some real hairy people were gunning for him, and then he winds up on a garbage dump, tied up and blindfolded so some chickenshit punk can shoot him in the back of the head."

"Well, the police are looking for them, aren't they?" she asked.

"Oh, sure. After a fashion, and for the wrong people for the wrong motives."

"What do you mean?"

"The heroin angle. I think the whole thing was a plant. And it worked, at least so far. They got just the situation they wanted: The sheriff's department in Coleville has jurisdiction because that's where it happened, but they're convinced the crime was committed by professional hoodlums from San Francisco. The San Francisco police will help as much as they can, but they're not about to run a temperature over a dead man in Nevada; they've got a dead man of their own—a whole morgue full of 'em and more coming in by the hour. We'll be in touch, fellas; how's the weather up there? And neither police force, Coleville *or* San Francisco, is going to start a crusade over a rubbed-out heroin dealer: Well, that's one son of a bitch we don't have to contend with anymore; they ought to do it more often."

"Then you think he was killed for that money he drew out of the bank? Somebody knew about it."

"No. He was forced to draw it out of the bank; and then the same people killed him. You can futz around with it until you're blue in the face, and you'll never make a case for his having drawn that money out voluntarily."

"You mean extortion?" she asked. "A threat of some kind?"

"Right."

"But how? They said he came into the bank alone. What was to keep him from calling the police?"

"Richter just has to be wrong about it, that's all. Somebody was covering him, and they missed it. What other forms of extortion are there? He was too tough to pay blackmail, even if they had something really serious on him, which I don't believe for a minute. Kidnap? I'm the only family he had, and nobody tried to kidnap me."

"Maybe they'd read 'The Ransom of Red Chief,'" she said.

"Smartass."

"How are you going to find out?"

"Go talk to Richter and Winegaard, to begin with."

"Did they teach you investigative techniques in the CIA? Or just interrogation—the iron maiden—bastinado?"

"Will you cut it out? CIA!"

"Didn't you know you talk in your sleep?"

"I do?"

"Scared you, didn't I? Well, you do, but it's always in Spanish. I've been thinking of enrolling at Berlitz."

"I'm probably talking to the other drivers; Berlitz doesn't teach that kind of Spanish. Anyway, why wouldn't I speak it? My mother was Cuban, and I lived in Havana most of the time until I was fourteen, when she died."

"I know. And then you gave up a career in professional baseball to become a stodgy old businessman in Latin America—"

"You'd be surprised how easy it is for a catcher hitting one sixty to give up a career in professional baseball."

"Stop interrupting me. And this was just before the Bay of Pigs. Odd, wasn't it?"

"If I plead guilty to all charges, can I make love to you again?"

"Well—"

"Now we're getting somewhere. Why didn't I think of copping out before? Did you know I also fomented the Boxer Rebellion and started the War of Jenkins' Ear?"

He arose a little before nine, showered and shaved as quietly as he could, and took a fresh suit and the rest of his clothes out into the living room to dress. This was accomplished with only one or two drowsy mutters from the depths of Mayo's pillow, largely undistinguishable except for something about a goddamned rhinoceros.

He expected to find the kitchen barren of anything edible, the way he'd left it when he had taken off for Baja California, but discovered she'd restocked it, at least for breakfast. He put on coffee, mixed some orange juice, and toasted a cinnamon roll in the broiler of the oven. It would be an hour yet before the bank opened, so he'd have time to talk to Winegaard first. He looked up the number and dialed. Yes, the secretary said, Mr. Winegaard was in and would be glad to see Mr. Romstead. In about fifteen minutes. He scribbled a note to Mayo saying he'd be back before noon and walked over to Montgomery Street. It was a sunny morning, at least downtown, but cool enough to be typical of San Francisco's summer.

There was a customer's room with a number of desks and big armchairs where men were watching stock quotations on a board, with the partners' offices at the rear of it. Edward Winegaard's was large and expensively carpeted, with a massive desk, and a mounted Pacific sailfish on one wall. Winegaard was a man near his father's age, trim and in good shape and tanned, with conservatively cut silvery hair. He arose to shake hands and indicated the armchair before his desk.

"It was a very tragic thing," he said. "And I don't understand it. I don't understand it at all."

"Neither do I," Romstead replied. "But all I've had so far is secondhand information, which is why I wanted to talk to you. You've known him for a long time?"

"Twenty—ah—twenty-seven years now."

"Then there's no question he made that money in the stock market?"

"None at all. Why?"

"The police seem to have some doubt of it."

"I don't see why. It was quite easy, looking at it in retrospect; anybody with a good job and a little money to invest every month could have done it. All he'd have to do is study stocks the way your father did." He smiled faintly, like a man remembering some golden age that was gone. "And get into the market when the Dow was in the two hundred to three hundred range, good solid shares were selling at five or six times earnings, and the big glamor issues were still to come.

"I first met him in New York in 1945. I'd just got out of the Army and was with Merrill Lynch. He had about twelve thousand dollars in savings and what I thought were very sound ideas on how he wanted to invest it. I've handled his business ever since. We had arguments, plenty of them—most of which he won—and I'll have to admit that more than half the time he was right.

"Traditionally, you think of shipmasters and seamen as shellbacks and old fogies about a century behind the times, but in the matter of investments Captain Romstead was oriented toward the future all the way. He believed in the new technology—electronics especially, computers, and aerospace. He'd been a radioman himself—"

"I didn't know that," Romstead said.

"Yes. You see, when he first got his officer's papers, he was

61

still sailing in Norwegian ships, before he became a U.S. citizen. And in those days it was quite common—as he explained it to me—for one of the mates of a Norwegian ship to double as wireless operator. So he had both tickets then.

"It was more or less natural then—especially after he started sailing out of here—for him to see the potentialities of the new electronics issues like Ampex, Varian, and Hewlett-Packard. He also bought IBM and Xerox at prices—and before multiple splits—that would make strong men break down and cry if you started talking about them now. And of course, shipmasters were making very good salaries by then; he was working steadily and buying more stock all the time. His portfolio was worth a million or a little over as far back as 1965."

"Good," Romstead said. "Now, for the second part—the pruning job when he liquidated that two hundred and fifty thousand. How does that jibe with your twenty-seven years' experience with him?"

"It doesn't," Winegaard said flatly. "As my grandchildren would say—no way."

"It was that bad?"

"A child with a pair of scissors could have done just as well." Winegaard took from his desk a list consisting of three pages clipped together. "This is a copy of our latest statement to him—that is, the shares we held for him in street name. What he did was simply to sell everything on the first page, except for one minor item at the bottom of it. Without going into detail about it, this included two issues we'd bought for him only the week before and that we were very high on, and another he'd had for less than a month and that was performing even better than we'd expected. It makes no sense at all that he would sell these.

"And on the next two pages there were three stocks we'd already more than halfway decided to unload. Approxi-

62

mately the same amount of money involved, around ninety thousand. I argued with him, or tried to, but he cut me off very abruptly. He didn't want to argue about it, he said. Sell at the market opening and deposit the proceeds in his checking account as soon as possible."

Romstead was conscious of growing excitement. Now they were getting somewhere. "Well, look—did he specifically mention the sum two hundred and fifty thousand as the amount he needed?"

"No, he didn't. He'd know, of course, from the previous closing quotations within a few thousand what the list would bring—barring some upheaval in the market overnight. Actually, the proceeds after commission came to something a little over two hundred and fifty-three thousand."

"And what was the item at the bottom of the first page that he didn't sell?"

"Some warrants. Fifteen hundred dollars altogether, around that."

"In other words, he completely ignored everything on the other two pages. And when you tried to bring up some stocks that were listed on these pages is when he cut you off?"

"Hmmmm, yes. That's about it."

"How did he sound to you? Was there anything unusual about his voice or mode of expression?"

"No. Not at all. Your father, let's face it, could be quite brusque and impatient when he wanted action instead of conversation."

"No," Romstead said. "I don't think that's the reason he cut you off."

"What do you mean?"

"I think he was being forced to liquidate those stocks, and the people who were leaning on him didn't know—for some reason—that there were two more pages. Otherwise, they'd have got it all."

"Good God! Do you think a thing like that is possible?"

"What other explanation can you think of?"

"But how could they hope to get the money? It would be in the bank. And bankers, before they cash checks for a quarter million dollars, are apt to ask for a little identification."

"No. They expected to get it in cash—which is exactly the way they did get it. Before they killed him."

The double glass doors of the Northern California First National Bank were at street level, and with the wide windows on each side it was possible for anyone to see the whole interior. It was high-ceilinged with ornate chandeliers and a waxed terrazzo floor. On the left, in front and extending more than halfway back, was a carpeted area behind a velvet rope which held the officers' desks. On the right in front was more of the terrazzo lobby extending to wide carpeted stairs leading downward, no doubt to the safe-deposit vaults. Beyond these areas there were tellers' windows on both sides, and then at the back a railing, several girls at bookkeeping machines, and the iron-grille doorway into the open vault. Down the center there were three chest-high writing stands with glass tops.

One uniformed guard was on duty at the desk at the head of the stairs to the safe-deposit vaults, and he could see another tidying up the forms at the rearmost of the writing stands. Three of the tellers' windows were open, and there were six or seven customers. This is where they did it, Romstead thought, in front of everybody. They had to be good. He went in.

Owen Richter's desk was just inside the entrance to the carpeted area. Richter himself was a slender graying man with an air of conservatism and unflappable competence, and Romstead was forced to concede it didn't seem likely the eyes behind those rimless glasses ever missed much that went on in the bank or were often fooled by what they saw. He introduced himself and explained why he was here. Richter shook his head.

"There's not a chance, Mr. Romstead. It's exactly as I told the police, and the executor—Bolling, isn't it? Your father, when he came in and picked up that money, was sober, entirely rational, and alone."

"He couldn't have been," Romstead said. "It was completely out of character, something he simply wouldn't do."

"Oh, as for that, I couldn't agree with you more. I've known Captain Romstead for close to ten years. He was very sound and conservative and highly competent in managing money. And because I did know him and knew this was totally unlike him, I was suspicious myself when he first telephoned me, that Monday before the withdrawal, and said he was going to want that amount of money in cash. It's irregular. And also foolish and highly dangerous. I tried to talk him out of it, but got nowhere. He simply said to expedite the clearance, that he wanted the money by Wednesday, and hung up.

"As you're probably aware, there are certain types of swindlers who prey on older people, and while I was sure the con man who'd pick your father for a victim would be making the mistake of his life, I made a note to be on the lookout when he came in, just to be sure there was no third party lurking in the background. I also alerted Mr. Wilkins, the security officer on duty in the main lobby here. He knew the captain by sight, of course."

"You don't know where he called from, that Monday?"

"No, he didn't say. And of course there's no way to tell; it came through the switchboard, and nowadays with long-distance dialing they wouldn't know either."

"He said he'd call back Wednesday to see if the deposit had cleared. Did you by any chance offer to call him?"

65

"Yes, I did. But he said not to bother; he'd call."

"And what time did he?"

"Around ten thirty Wednesday morning. I told him clearance had just come through, so he said he would be in in about ten minutes."

"Did he specify any denominations for the money?" Romstead asked.

"Yes. In fifties and hundreds. I gave instructions to have it counted out and ready for him in the vault. As you'll see, from my desk here I can see the whole lobby, from the vault on out to the front doors, and even the sidewalk outside, through the windows. I told Mr. Wilkins he would be here in a few minutes, so he was on the lookout, too. I think it was just ten forty exactly when your father came in."

"Was there anybody behind him?" Romstead asked.

"No. Not immediately behind him. By the time he'd walked over to my desk there was another man came in, but I knew him. He owns a restaurant down the street and has been a bank customer for years. The captain came on over to the desk here. He was carrying a small bag—"

"Do you remember what kind it was?" Romstead interrupted. "And what color?"

"Gray. It was just the common type of airplane luggage you can buy anywhere, even in drugstores. I asked him to sit down, but he refused; he seemed to be impatient to get on with the transaction. I tried again to tell him how dangerous it was, carrying that much money around the streets, but he waved me off rather abruptly. So I told him if he'd write out the check, I'd go back to the vault and get the money for him, but he said he'd go with me. Mr. Wilkins came over, and the three of us walked back. The captain took out his checkbook and stopped at one of the stands out there to write the check and sign it. We went on to the railing there outside the vault, and I asked to have the money

66

brought out. It was banded, of course, and the captain accepted our count as we put it in the bag. He thanked me, and Mr. Wilkins and I walked to the front door with him."

"And nobody followed him out?"

"No. We were particularly on the lookout for that, but it was a minute or two before anybody else went out, and again it was a customer I knew. I still didn't like the transaction, so I stepped out on the sidewalk myself just to be sure there was nobody waiting for him outside. He went up to the corner, waited for the light, and crossed Montgomery. He was still alone, nobody following him."

Romstead glumly shook his head. "Well, that seems to be it."

"Yes, there's not a chance in the world he was being threatened or coerced in any way. All the time he was here at my desk he could have told me without being overheard. And back there by the vault Mr. Wilkins and I were both alone with him. Also, when he crossed Montgomery, he passed right in front of a police car, stopped for the light."

But, damn it, Romstead thought, it *had* to be. There was no other answer. "How many people were in the lobby altogether?"

"Several came in and went out during the whole period, but I don't think there were ever more than eight at one time."

"Was there anybody who was strange to you? Who wasn't a customer and you couldn't remember seeing before?"

"Yes. There were two." The answer was unhesitating and precise. "One was a young woman with blond hair, wearing dark glasses. I think she was buying travelers' checks. The other was a hippie type with a big bushy beard, a headband, and hair down to his shoulders. He was wearing one of those poncho things and had a guitar slung over his shoulder."

"What was he doing? He doesn't sound much like a regular bank customer."

"He was counting his change. I guess he'd been panhandling." Distaste was evident in Richter's tone. "He came in just a few minutes before the captain and was at that middle stand there with a double handful of nickels, dimes, and quarters spread out on it, counting them."

"He didn't have one hand under the poncho, any TV routine like that?"

"Oh, no. Anyway, he was still here after the captain went out. He was at one of the tellers' windows. Getting currency for all that silver, I suppose."

"I just don't get it," Romstead said. "There's only one thing that strikes me as a little odd. You asked him to sit down here and write the check, but he refused. Then he stopped at one of the stands and wrote it. Didn't he have a pen?"

"Oh, I offered him one."

"Did it strike you as strange?"

"No-o. Not really. It was my impression, I think, that he didn't want me to go after the money—that is, it'd be quicker if he went too."

"Well, when he stopped to write it on the way back to the vault, was it the stand where the hippie was?"

"No. It was the one at the rear."

"Then the hippie couldn't have seen the amount?"

"No, not unless he had exceptional eyesight—" Richter stopped, his eyes thoughtful. "Yes, he might have. As I recall now, he finished his counting and had gathered up his silver while your father was writing out the check, and he went past on the other side of the stand, going to one of the tellers' windows. But I don't think that's significant; he could just as easily have seen, or guessed, what the three of us were doing back there by the vault with the bag, if he had robbery

68

in mind. Anyway, as I said, he was still in the bank after your father left."

Romstead walked back to the apartment, feeling baffled and frustrated. How could he be right and wrong at the same time?

VI

"IF the first supposition is right, then the second one has to be too," he told Mayo. "Richter missed it, and now I've missed it; but it still has to be there."

"Not necessarily," she replied. She was wearing the housecoat and a pair of mules, but she'd combed her hair and put on lipstick. She was perched crosswise in a big armchair in the living room, sipping coffee. "You're projecting your hypothesis from an opinion, not a known fact, when you say it couldn't have been kidnap. It could have been a girl-friend."

"A quarter million dollars?"

"Men as tough and as promiscuous as your father have turned out to be vulnerable, the same as anybody else, thousands of times. In which case he'd have come in alone to get the money. It wouldn't have been voluntary, by any stretch of the imagination, but they wouldn't have to be there."

"No." He shook his head. "You're missing the key to the whole thing. They wouldn't have had to be there to force him to sell the stock either. You ever hear of kidnappers coming in to discuss the thing in person? The threat comes by note or telephone. We couldn't care less how you raise the money, Jack; just raise it."

"But you don't know they were there. Opinion again."

"Yes, they were there. He wasn't alone when he was talking to Winegaard; that's implicit in the whole conversation.

70

There are two phones in that house, one in the master bedroom and a wall-mounted extension in the kitchen, and one of the bastards was listening in while the others applied the pressure.

"Look—in kidnap *or* blackmail, a specific sum is demanded, and you raise it to suit yourself within the time limit. That being the case, he would have sold selectively, or at least he'd have let Winegaard express an opinion. But he wasn't trying to raise a specific sum; he was selling a list of stocks with a gun against his head, knowing Winegaard was going to protest in a minute and he had to shut him up before he could mention some stocks that weren't on the list."

She nodded thoughtfully. "Yes, I guess that's right."

"Sure. And utterly pointless, so far. After they'd done all that, there was no way in Christ's world they could get the money. Except that they did."

"Well, what are you going to do now?"

He considered. At the moment he could see two possible leads, both very tenuous and both calling for a hell of a lot of legwork. One was Jeri Bonner, and the other the Mercedes. He couldn't explore both avenues at once, so the best thing would be to get some help doing the bloodhounding and backtracking here while he went back to Nevada. He had an idea about the car, something Brubaker had overlooked or dismissed as unimportant, and he had a hunch he could find the place. It would just take a lot of driving. He'd had enough of that highway up through Sacramento and across the Sierra, so he'd fly up and rent a car in Reno. He told her.

"When will you be back?" she asked.

"Tomorrow night, probably."

"Can I go too?"

"No."

"Why not?"

71

"That desert's hotter than the floor plates of hell. And you'd just be bored, and choked with dust—"

"Spare me the bullshit, Romstead. I can't go because it might be dangerous, right?"

"Dangerous? Of course not."

"You're looking for a place, but you don't have the faintest idea what the place consists of or who's going to be there. If it's the people who killed your father, they'll invite you in for a drink—"

"I don't intend to carry a sign."

"So of course they'll think you're the Avon lady. Or you could disguise yourself as a jockey. You and your goddamned CIA. . . . I might as well get dressed and go home." She got up and flounced out of the room but reappeared in the doorway a moment later, looking contrite and worried. "You will be careful, won't you?"

"Sure," Romstead said. He brought out his address book and looked up Jeff Loring's number. Loring was a college classmate who'd been with the FBI for a while and now was practicing law in San Francisco. They'd had lunch together a couple of times in the months Romstead had been in town. Loring was in, and if the question surprised him, he concealed it.

"Private investigator? Sure, I know several, personally or by reputation, but they specialize a lot: divorce, skip tracing, background investigation, security—"

"Skip tracing, in that area. General police experience."

"Murdock sounds like your man. Larry Murdock. He runs a small agency on Post Street. I haven't got his number handy, but you can get it from the book."

"Thanks a lot, Jeff. I'll tell you about it later."

"No sweat. Give me a call, and we'll have lunch."

He looked up the number and dialed. He introduced himself and said he was calling on Loring's recommendation.

72

"I'd come there, but I've got some more phone calls to make." He gave the address. "Could you send one of your men over?"

"I'll come myself," Murdock replied. "Half hour be all right?"

"That'll be fine."

Mayo came out dressed for the street while he was looking up the Nevada area code. "You want me to call about flight times?" she asked.

"Yeah, if you would, honey. I'll be tied up here for the next couple of hours."

She leaned down to kiss him and went out. Her apartment was in another building of the same complex.

He called directory assistance in area code 702 for Mrs. Carmody's number and dialed, praying she'd be in. The information he could give Murdock would be sketchy until he could get hold of her. Carmelita answered. Mrs. Carmody was out by the pool. One moment, please.

"Eric? Where in the world are you? I thought you went back to San Francisco."

"That's where I'm calling from. How are you?"

"Fine. But still a little shook about Jeri."

"I know. But she's why I called. Do you by any chance know what her address was here? Or where she worked?"

"No-o. I don't think I ever did. The only person who would know would be Lew, but for God's sake, don't tackle him. I know what you're trying to do—"

"Right. It's almost a cinch there was something between her and the old man. And Bonner suspected it. Remember, he was bitter as hell even before he knew she was dead, there in the house."

"Well," she said hesitantly, "that's right. But it wasn't entirely over Jeri."

"I understand." He'd suspected that already; Bonner had

a thing for Paulette Carmody himself and was jealous. Sister and girlfriend both, he thought; it was no wonder he hated the name Romstead. "It seems to me he'd have been one of Brubaker's prime suspects."

"Oh, he might have been except he was in his store until two o'clock that morning and then in a poker game with five or six other men until after daylight. No, it wasn't Lew. He's violent and pugnacious as hell, but straightforward about it. If he'd done it, it would have been on the steps of city hall in front of two hundred witnesses. Which is why I said don't even think of calling him about Jeri. He's out on bail now for beating a man almost to death in a bar last night. Some ranch hand he overheard say something about Jeri and Captain Romstead."

"Don't worry," Romstead said. "I intend to give him all the room he needs. . . . Well, could you give me a description of her?"

"She was about five feet five, around a hundred and ten pounds. Blue eyes, dark-red hair, nose just a little on the baby side, but cute. Leggy for a girl who wasn't very tall."

"Good. You don't know what type of work she did?"

"Clerical. She'd had some business courses—typing and so on—at San Diego State. Wait—I just remembered something. Last winter she bought Lew a tape deck at employee discount; she was working for some electronics supply outfit."

"You can't recall the name?"

"No, I'm sorry. But it seems to me he said it was on Mission Street."

"Fine. That's enough for a start. Thanks a million."

After he'd hung up, he remembered something else he'd intended to ask her. It was about the crewman the old man had turned over to the narcs for having heroin aboard his ship. Until you had a solid lead to follow, you had to consider everything a possibility. Well, he'd call her tomorrow from up there.

He brought out a bag and began to pack. The phone rang. It was Mayo. There was a flight at three o'clock, with space available. He asked her to make the reservation for him.

"Okay. I'll drive you to the airport."

"You're an angel."

"With an angel's sex life. I might as well be having an affair with a whaler."

Just as he hung up, the doorbell chimed.

Larry Murdock was a lean-faced man in his middle forties with coolly watchful gray eyes and an air of quietness about him. He introduced himself and produced a wallet-sized photostat of his license. Romstead closed the door and they sat down.

"You've had police experience, no doubt?" he asked.

"Yes. Fifteen years, here in San Francisco. What is it you want done, Mr. Romstead?"

"Just more of the same. Ringing doorbells and asking questions. I'm trying to backtrack two people to see if they knew each other, and how well, and what other people they knew. It'll probably go faster with two men on it, if you've got somebody available. Okay?"

"Yes. I think we can handle it." Murdock took a notebook from a pocket of his jacket and unclipped a pen.

"Fine. There's a lot of background you'll need." Romstead told him the whole thing, from the discovery of his father's body to and including his interviews with Winegaard and Richter. He wound up with descriptions of his father and Jeri Bonner and the address of his father's apartment on Stockton Street. Murdock listened without interruption, now and then taking notes.

"I don't think he was ever in the apartment in that period from the sixth to the fourteenth, but I haven't seen the build-

75

ing and don't know what the setup is in regard to privacy of access," he concluded. "But you can see what I'm after."

"Sure. Whether anybody at all saw him around the place, whether he was alone if they did, and if the girl had ever been seen in the area or with him. Since it's all right with you, I'll start another man checking out the girl, beginning with the electronics supply places."

"Good. Personally, I think she was on the lam from something or somebody, or she wouldn't have gone home. She was a junkie, and her chances of making a connection in that town would be close to zero."

"Yes. Unless her sources had dried up here and she remembered that deck stashed in your father's place."

"That's a possibility, of course," Romstead conceded. "But there's another thing about that I can't quite buy."

"I think I know what you mean," Murdock said. "If she knew about it at all, why didn't she know it was uncut? So why the OD?"

"Right," Romstead replied. "Maybe she didn't run far enough." He was beginning to have a solid respect for the other man. He went over to the desk by the window and wrote out a check for three hundred dollars. "I'll be in Coleville tonight, and I'll give you a call."

Murdock thanked him for the retainer and left. Romstead finished packing the bag, put in his binoculars, and called Mayo. She was ready. He carried the bag down to her car. They swung up onto the freeway and headed out Bayshore. The car was a new Mustang, and she handled it with cool competence. He relaxed, which he seldom did when someone else was driving.

"Very flattering," she said, passing Candlestick Park.

"What?"

"When a man keeps his eyes on your legs instead of traffic. Sort of overall endorsement."

76

"Well, you are a good driver," he agreed. "That's why they wouldn't let you in medical school."

"And the legs?"

"They're why you didn't need to get into medical school."

"Chauvinist pig."

It was overcast at the airport with a chill wind whipping the bay and fog pushing in over the hills above South City like rolls of cotton batting. She had to double park at the unloading zone. "Call me," she said.

"Tonight."

"And tomorrow." They kissed, and she clung to him tightly for a moment until the inevitable horn sounded behind them. He lifted out the bag and watched her drive off. He went inside, checked in, and paid for his ticket with a credit card. The flight was only a little late in taking off, and they were down in Reno's heat shortly after 4 P.M. He rented an air-conditioned Chevrolet, asked for a Nevada highway map, and drove into town.

Finding a place to park, he unfolded the map. Coleville was in Steadman County, but only fifteen miles from the boundary of Garnet County, adjoining it on the south. He'd need both to give him a radius of twenty-five miles all the way around. He looked up a sporting goods store and bought the two large-scale county maps of the type put out for hunters and fishermen. "Better give me a gallon water cooler, too," he told the clerk.

Traffic was heavy now, and it was slow going until he was past the outskirts of town. He took time out for some dinner at a highway truck stop, and it was a little before eight when he pulled into Coleville. He parked under the porte cochere at the Conestoga Motel and went inside.

A rather sour-faced man of middle age was at the desk this time and checked him in without a smile of any kind, commercial or otherwise. He drove back with the key and let himself into room 16. Unfolding the two maps on the bed, side by side in their proper orientation, he pulled up a chair and bent over them with a frown of concentration.

No doubt Brubaker was right in that there were countless miles of tracks and old ruts out through the sagebrush flats and that checking them all out would have been a hopeless task from the start, but the car hadn't been on any of these. The significant fact wasn't merely that it was covered with dust, but that the dust was unmarred by streaks along the sides as it inevitably would have been in running through brush. It had been on a graded road, which narrowed the possible routes immensely.

The roads were coded on the maps: paved highways, gravel, and graded dirt roads. Gravel, of course, could be almost as dusty as plain dirt, so he'd have to cover those too. The main highway, which he'd just come in on, ran roughly north and south. This was crossed in town, at Third Street, by an east-west blacktop, the road his father's place was on. Beyond the old man's house it continued on westward for another twenty or thirty miles to a small community on a lake, but there were no unpaved roads leading off it. So it had to be north, south, or east of town. From that fifty-four miles unaccounted for on the odometer you had to subtract four for the old man's return home after having the car serviced. That left fifty miles round trip from the house, or forty-two miles round trip from the center of town.

South on the highway there were two possibilities. About thirteen miles out the pavement was crossed by a gravel road running east and west. North there were also two, twelve miles out and sixteen, both dirt roads taking off in a generally westerly direction. East there were three. Nine miles from town a graded dirt road left the blacktop running north, and after about four miles it forked, one branch veering off to the northeast. Also, at about seventeen miles from

78

town another gravel road left the pavement in a southerly direction. Out and back each time, if he had to cover all of them, added up to 108 miles of chuckholed and dusty off-the-pavement driving. It was going to be a long day. He rang the office and left a call for five thirty in the morning.

Dialing the long distance operator, he put in the call to Mayo. She apparently grabbed the phone up on the first ring, and it was obvious from her voice that something was wrong.

"Eric! I've been poised over this phone for hours!"

"What is it?"

"Your apartment's been burglarized. I didn't know what motel you were in, so all I could do was wait—"

"All right, honey, just simmer down; he probably didn't get much. But how do you know?"

"*Know?* How do I know? Eric, I'm trying to tell you. I talked to him—I walked right in on him—"

He broke in swiftly. "Are you hurt?"

"No. He didn't do anything at all. I pretended to believe him."

He sighed softly. Thank God for a smart girl. "Okay, Crafty, just start from the beginning."

"All right." She took a deep breath. "On the way back from the airport I decided while I had the car out I might as well do some grocery shopping, and I bought some things for you too—a steak and a bottle of rosé and some tonic water, oh, a bagful of stuff. After I'd put mine away, I thought I'd take yours over and tidy up the apartment a little. So I went over and took the elevator up, and when I opened the door, I almost dropped the bag and my purse and everything. There was a man standing right there in the living room, with a kind of tool bag open on the rug. But it was funny—I mean, I was scared blue, but he didn't seem to be startled at all. With my arms full like that I must

79

have fumbled around for maybe fifteen seconds getting the door open—I had the wrong key at first—so he had some warning. He just smiled and said, 'Good afternoon, are you Mrs. Romstead?' and leaned down to get something out of the tool kit.

"By then I'd got my heart down out of my throat and could speak, so I asked him what he was doing there. He took a slip of paper out of a breast pocket—he had on a white coverall—and said, 'Mr. Romstead called us to check out the simalizer and put a new frammistat in his KLH.' That wasn't what he actually said, of course, but some technical jargon that didn't mean a thing to me, and he had the console of the KLH pulled out from the wall as if he were going to work on it. He said the manager let him in, which I knew was a damn lie—the office wouldn't let anybody in an apartment when the tenant's not there—but I didn't know what to do. If I started to run, he might grab me and drag me inside to keep me from calling the police.

"And, believe me, I didn't want to go on into the kitchen with those groceries, either, because then he'd be between me and the door, but there didn't seem to be anything else I could do without making him suspicious. He'd know I'd opened the door for something. Anyway, he was so cool and professional that by then I'd about decided he really was an honest, card-carrying burglar and not a creep of some kind, so I told him I was just a friend that had stopped by with this stuff for you. So I went into the kitchen and shoved the things in the refrigerator—I mean, all of it, and fast, in case you ever wonder why there's a package of paper napkins and two bars of toilet soap in your freezer. I came back out. He was humming under his breath and fiddling with the back of the KLH. I said something about being sure the door was locked when he left and eased out. I didn't think my knees would ever hold up till I made it to the elevator.

"When I got to the office, of course, I had to explain what the hell *I* was doing in your apartment. We got that straightened out, and they called the police. A squad car pulled up in two or three minutes, and the manager went up with the two officers. He was gone by then, of course, but they found enough evidence he'd been there so they didn't write me off as some kind of nut. It seemed to be your desk he was interested in—or that's as far as he'd got—because everything in it had been pretty well shuffled. Of course, they don't know if anything's missing, but they said the chances were he got the hell out of there the minute I was out of the corridor."

Alarm circuits were tripping all over the place, but he was merely soothing—and admiring. "Honey, you handled it beautifully; you really used your head. Anyway, there was nothing in the desk but correspondence, old tax returns, bank statements, and so on. Could you describe the guy?"

"He wasn't real big, a little less than six feet, anyway, around a hundred and sixty pounds. About thirty years old. Very slender and dark, Indian-looking, with black hair and brown eyes. And cool, real cool."

"Well, you're pretty cool yourself, Hotshot," Romstead said. While he didn't like any of it, he still didn't want to scare her over what so far was just a feeling. "But don't let it go to your head. If there are prowlers working those apartments, keep the chain on your door the way I told you, and don't let *anybody* in until you've finished the first two volumes of his biography. I'll call you tomorrow, and I'll be back early tomorrow night."

They talked a few minutes more, and as soon as he'd hung up, he put in a call to Murdock. His answering service said Mr. Murdock wasn't at his office or at home yet, but

81

that he should report in shortly. Romstead gave her the number of the motel. "Ask him to call me as soon as he comes in."

All he could do then was wait. And wonder about it. Too many things were wrong with the picture. Naturally, any prowler could get names off the mailboxes down below, but this guy wasn't some punk who'd wandered in off the street with a strip of plastic or a credit card. He couldn't have got in. Those were dead-bolt locks, and he'd turned the key when he left. Then there were the other touches, the coverall, the prop toolbag—both disposable down the nearest garbage chute—the calm assurance, the plausible patter, all of which bespoke a real professional—except that no professional in his right mind would waste his time prowling a single man's apartment, even if you left him a key under the doormat. No furs, no jewelry—all the expensive baubles belonged to women. He'd get three or four suits that some fence might give him two dollars apiece for and the cleaning woman's eight dollars if he could find it.

He could call Paulette Carmody, but he didn't want to have the phone tied up if Murdock called. He waited. He unpacked his bag and studied the maps some more. It was about twenty minutes before the phone rang. He grabbed it up. It was Murdock.

"I just got your call," he said. "Anything new?"

"Yeah, some guy shook down my apartment this afternoon," Romstead replied. "I can't figure what he was after, but let's take up your end of it first. You get any line on the girl?"

"Yes, we've had pretty good luck so far. I've just talked to Snyder again—he's the man I put on her. He picked up her trail at Packer Electronics right off the bat. It's a big outfit on upper Mission, handles everything in the electronics line: hi-fi components, radio and TV parts and tubes, transistors, ham equipment, and so on. She worked in the office there for about a year and a half, until last March. They let her go for tapping the till; apparently her habit was pretty expensive even then. Snyder got her last known address and checked that out. She'd been sharing an apartment with another girl named Sylvia Wolden out near the Marina, but she'd moved out of there in April. The Wolden girl didn't know she was on junk but suspected she was shoplifting, from the things she'd bring home.

"She left no forwarding address, but Sylvia was able to give Snyder the name of an old boyfriend, Leo Cullen, who tends bar at a place on Van Ness. Cullen told Snyder he'd broken up with her along about Christmas, when she first got hooked on the stuff, and hadn't seen her since but had heard she was shacked up with a guy named Marshall Tallant, who ran a one-man TV repair place in North Beach. Snyder went out there and found the place; but it was closed, and nobody in the neighborhood had seen Tallant in over a month. The girl had been living with him, though, and they'd both disappeared from the neighborhood about the same time."

"Any idea how she was supporting her habit?" Romstead asked. "Tallant couldn't have made much out of that shop."

"No," Murdock replied. "We haven't got any line on that yet. If she was hustling, it apparently wasn't in that neighborhood, though she might have been shoplifting downtown. And you're right about the shop—Tallant couldn't have paid for any forty- or fifty-dollar habit unless he had other sources of income. I gather he was plenty good, could fix anything electronic, but snotty and temperamental. He'd turn down jobs if they didn't interest him, and some days he didn't even open the place.

"There's one possibility, though, and that brings me to my end of it. She could have had some kind of hustle going with your father. What, I don't know, but she definitely had been in his apartment a good many times. Three people I talked to had seen her going in or coming out of the building over the past four months, but never with him. She might have been working as a high-priced call girl, with him as one of her list; I just don't know. But I do think she had a key. One of the tenants I talked to saw her in the corridor on that floor on the Fourth of July, and you remember your father was in Coleville then. And I think it's definite your father was never in the apartment any time between July sixth and fourteenth. Nobody saw him at all, not even the apartment house manager, and he and your father were good friends. He's a retired merchant marine man himself, mate on a Standard Oil tanker, and when your father came to town, they always had a couple of drinks together.

"But here's the strange part of it. You're not the only one interested in her. There's another guy; Snyder crossed his trail twice, and I saw him myself when he came to the apartment house. And that's not all. Unless Snyder and I both are watching too much cloak-and-dagger on TV, this guy himself had a tail on him. We were a whole damn procession shuttling around town."

"Are you sure of this?" Romstead asked.

"We're sure of the guy; the tail's only a guess. He was right ahead of Snyder at the electronics place and then came into the bar on Van Ness—where Cullen worked—while Snyder was still there. Real bruiser, big as you are but mean-looking, apparently just been in a fight. Had a cut place over one eye and a swollen right hand—"

"Wait," Romstead interrupted. "Driving a green Porsche with Nevada plates?"

"That's right. Then you know him?"

"I've met him. He's her brother, Lew Bonner. I don't get it, though, why he's poking into it. He had it all worked out;

my old man was to blame for everything that happened to her. But what about the tail?"

"As I say, we're not sure. Could be just a coincidence, but seeing him in Bonner's area three times in different parts of town is stretching it. Name's Delevan; he used to be in the business but had his license yanked and did a stretch in San Quentin for extortion—"

"Can you describe him?" Romstead cut in quickly.

"He's pretty hefty himself, about six two, over two hundred pounds, partially bald—"

"Okay," Romstead said. "He's not the one."

"That shook down your apartment, you mean? When did it happen?"

"Just after I took off for Reno. I think he must have clocked me out, made sure I was on the plane, and then came back and let himself in." Romstead told him the whole thing. He was puzzled also.

"Sounds pro to me, too, but what the hell would he be after? That's a furnished apartment, isn't it?"

"The only things in it that are mine are clothes, luggage, and that hi-fi gear and some records."

"Planting a bug, maybe?"

"I thought of that, but why? They wouldn't know I'm interested in them. I didn't know it myself until this morning. You haven't got a description on Tallant?"

"No, but I can get one damned fast. Let me call you back in about ten minutes."

"Fine." Romstead hung up, frowning. What was Bonner doing in San Francisco, checking back on Jeri? Had he held out on Brubaker or learned something new? He waited, consumed with impatience. When the phone rang, he snatched it up.

"I just called Snyder," Murdock said, "and he checked back with one of the people he'd talked to in North Beach.

Tallant's about thirty or thirty-two, medium height, slender, black hair, brown eyes—"

"That's enough," Romstead cut in. "Have you got an extra man you can get hold of this time of night?"

"Sure. You want Miss Foley covered?"

"Like a blanket, every minute till I get back there. I don't know what the son of a bitch is up to or what he had to do with the old man, but he sounds wrong as hell to me."

"We'll take care of it. What's her apartment number? And description?"

Romstead told him. "That retainer I gave you won't begin to cover this, but for references you can check the Wells Fargo Bank on Montgomery Street or the Southland Trust in San Diego."

"That's all right. You're coming back tomorrow?"

"Sometime tomorrow. I guess I should have stayed there; that seems to be where it is. But as long as I'm up here, I might as well go ahead and finish what I started to do. Don't let her out of your sight. And see what else you can find out about Tallant."

After he'd hung up, he debated whether to call Mayo again but decided there was no point in getting her upset over something that could be miles into left field. He had complete confidence in Murdock, anyway.

He called Paulette Carmody's number. She was out, playing bridge, Carmelita said, and would be back around midnight. Well, he could talk to her tomorrow.

VII

IT was full daylight when Romstead emerged from Logan's Café on Aspen Street after a breakfast of scrambled eggs, orange juice, and two cups of coffee and got into the rented car. He had put on lightweight slacks and a sport shirt, and the water cooler was filled and stowed on the floor behind the front seat. Beside him on the front seat were the Steadman County map and his 8 x 30 Zeiss binoculars. He read the odometer and jotted the mileage on the map: 6327.4. The street was almost deserted, the traffic lights flashing amber in the still-cool air of early morning as he drove out of town, headed south.

The sky was growing pink in the east, the same as it had been that morning two days ago, when he passed the cemetery. He glanced toward it, his face impassive, and went on. He thought of Jeri Bonner and wondered if her funeral would be today. All the unanswerable questions started invading his mind again, but he shut them out. He didn't intend to spend the day guessing and theorizing from the meager facts he had; too many of them were contradictory, and he was here to do something else, a specific task that might turn out to be futile but still had to be done.

In a few minutes the peaks of the Sierra, far off to his right, began to be tipped with yellow sunlight. The two-lane blacktop, which in reality was a good three lanes wide, ran straight down a wide valley floored with sage and rimmed with buttes and ridges on both sides. Ahead and behind there was nobody else in sight. He bore down on the accelerator until he was cruising at seventy.

He began to watch the odometer, but he saw the gravel road a good mile before he reached it. He turned right into it, stopped, and read the mileage: 6341.1. He subtracted and wrote 13.7 on the map at the juncture of the two roads. Eight miles each direction would cover it. He looked behind and then ahead. You could see almost the full eight miles both ways, he thought. He cranked the windows up, opened the wings a crack, and went on. It wasn't hot enough yet to need the air conditioning.

The road was badly washboarded and chuckholed, and he had to keep his speed down. A boiling cloud of dust rolled up behind, and he was thankful there was nobody ahead of him. Gravel roared against the underside of the car. A sage hen ran across the road, and several times he saw jackrabbits bounding out through the sage, raising and lowering their great ears like semaphores; but there was no sign of human habitation anywhere. After five miles he topped a low ridge and saw another immense flat spread out ahead of him. He stopped and got out to study it with the glasses. The road ran straight on, diminishing in the distance. There was no house, no shed, windmill, or structure of any kind. There was no use going any farther in this direction. Wherever his father had gone or had been taken, there had to be a habitation of some kind.

He turned around and drove back to the highway. Checking the mileage there, he continued on east on the gravel for eight miles. Nothing. He returned to the highway again and drove back to town. As he went past the motel, he wanted to stop and call Mayo but knew it was too early. It wasn't even eight o'clock yet; she wouldn't be up.

Traffic was still light in the streets, but the signals were in operation now. Stopped at Third Street, he checked the odometer and wrote the new reading on the map: 6380.8. He went on through town and out the highway, north this time. A few cars were abroad now, and he passed a couple of big diesel rigs. In about ten minutes he came to the first of the dirt roads leading off to the west. He had to wait for an oncoming car to turn left into it. He stopped, checked his mileage again, and entered it on the map: 6391.1.

The road curved down a slight grade and across a flat, rough and corrugated and full of axle-breaking chuckholes for the unwary, maintained for pickup trucks. Dust boiled up behind him. He checked the rearview mirror and could see nothing at all through the swirling white cloud. An old pickup came clattering toward him and passed, and he had to slow to a crawl until the dust of its passage began to settle. There was no wind at all, and it was growing hot now. He switched on the air conditioner. After eight miles on the odometer he topped another ridge and stopped. He got out with the glasses.

The road swung down from the ridge and turned north up another sagebrush flat. In the distance he could see a clump of cottonwoods, a corral, and tiny ranch buildings. At least four more miles, he thought. Too far, even allowing for slight differences in the odometers of the two cars. He turned and went back to the highway, picked up his new mileage reading, and continued north to the second road. It was only a dusty and monotonous repetition of the first. When his odometer reading added up first to twenty-one, and then twenty-two from town, he stopped and turned around.

He drove back to town and parked in front of his unit at the motel. When he got out, he saw the car was as dusty now as the Mercedes had been. He went inside and put through a call to Mayo. There was no answer. He let the phone go on ringing for a full minute before he gave up and broke the connection, uneasy in spite of himself. Hell, there was nothing to worry about. Wherever she'd gone, Murdock's man was right with her.

He called Murdock's office. Mr. Murdock was out, the receptionist said. So was Mr. Snyder. He identified himself and asked if there were any word from the man assigned to Miss Foley.

"No," the girl said, "he hasn't called in since he took over at eight. But he wouldn't, anyway, unless he'd lost her."

He was forced to admit this was right. Reassured, he thanked her and hung up. He dialed for a local line and called Paulette Carmody. She answered herself.

"Oh, Eric? You caught me just as I was going out the door."

"I'm sorry," he said. "I'll call back later."

"Oh, that's all right. It's the church service for Jeri, but I've got a few minutes. What is it?"

"Nothing important. It was just about that crew member you said the old man locked up for having heroin on the ship—"

"Oh, that kooky radio officer. Was *he* ever out there in space? Look—where are you now?"

"Here in Coleville. At the Conestoga."

"Fine. Honey, I'll be home all afternoon; why don't you come out for a drink and I'll tell you about the dingaling? It's quite a story."

"I'll be there," he said.

"Bye now."

He hung up. *Radio officer?* Then he shook his head angrily and went out to the car; there was no use indulging in any wild speculation until he had more than that to go on. Finish the job first, he told himself; find the place or admit you were wrong. He wrote the odometer reading on the map, drove up Aspen, turned right on Third Street, and was on the blacktop road headed east out of town.

The country was rougher in this direction, flinty hills and ridges and twisting ravines. The sun was high overhead now, and heat waves shimmered off the pavement. He came to the dirt road leading north and pulled off into it. A weathered signpost bore arrow markers saying KENDALL MTN 19 and LADYSMITH SPRGS 22. He checked the odometer and wrote 9.2 on the map. The road went up over a ridge and along a high flat with ravines on both sides. It was as rough as the others, the dust a grayish white and as fine as talcum. It was impossible to see anything behind him.

He came to the fork and stopped to read the mileage again: 13.4. He entered it on the map. The old signs, gouged and riddled with gunshots, indicated the road bearing off to the right led to Ladysmith Springs. He shrugged. It didn't matter which he took first. A pickup truck came into view down the other, leaving a swirling plume of dust behind it. The driver lifted a hand, and it went on past toward the highway. Romstead took the Ladysmith road and went on. After about a mile there was a small fenced enclosure on his left and a shed that had probably been used for the storage of winter hay in the past but was now empty and falling in ruin. After that there was nothing but sage and rock and powdery dust and the endless succession of low hills. When the odometer indicated he'd come twenty-three miles and there was still nothing in sight, he stopped, poured a drink of the water, waited a minute for his own dust to settle, and turned back.

He checked his mileage again at the fork and turned up the Kendall Mountain road, discouraged now and facing defeat. This was his next to last chance. The road ran for two or three miles up a shallow canyon, and when it climbed out, there was a fence on his right. The fence continued as

91

the road went up over another ridge and out across several miles of rough mesa, still running north. As his mileage was beginning to run out on him, he passed a gate through the fence, a wooden gate on high posts, with a single-lane road leading through it and disappearing over a slight rise about two hundred yards away. The fence turned at right angles shortly after the gate and ran off to the east across a continuation of the low ridge.

He was twenty-two miles from town when the road began to drop down from the mesa and he could see out across another wide flat ahead. There was no habitation visible anywhere. He noted the odometer reading and turned and went back. It was three miles to the gate. Nineteen miles from town, he thought. He stopped and got out.

The sun was straight overhead now, incandescent and searing in the cloudless sky, and its weight was like a blow after the cool interior of the car. There was still no wind, and in the boundless hush his shoes made little plopping sounds in the dust as he walked over to the gate. It was secured with a length of heavy chain and a rusty padlock that looked as though it hadn't been opened in years. He could see traces of tire treads in the dust on the other side, however, indistinct and half-obliterated by the desert's afternoon winds. They might have been made months ago. There was no way he could get through with the car, but he could walk out to where the road disappeared over the little rise and see what was in view from there. He lifted the binoculars off the seat, crawled through the three-strand fence, and walked up beside the road. As the country beyond began to come into view, he felt a little surge of excitement.

It was a wide bowl-shaped valley or flat, and on the far side of it, among a half dozen aspens or cottonwoods, was a ranch house. He lifted the binoculars and studied it. Besides the house itself, there was a barn, a smaller shed of

92

some kind, a corral, and off a short distance to one side a windmill and a large water tank. He breathed softly. It was a good two miles, he estimated, feeling conviction take hold of him, plus the nineteen to the gate would make it exactly right. But was there anybody there now?

No vehicle of any kind was visible, and he could see no one anywhere. Of course, there might be a car or a truck in the shed or around behind the house, but he didn't think so. Those tire marks in the road were too old. He swung the glasses onto the windmill again. Several of its blades appeared to be missing, but he couldn't be sure at this distance. He couldn't tell whether there was any water in the tank or not. But there were no animals in sight, no dog, chickens, horses, or anything, not even range cattle.

His eye was caught then by movement in the sage a quarter mile in front of the house, and he brought the glasses around. It was vultures, five or six of them clustered around something on the ground. As he watched, one of them took off, flapping, and began to soar. Two or three more were circling high overhead. He returned to his scrutiny of the ranch buildings. The place, he decided, was almost surely abandoned. There was no mailbox out here at the road, no telephone or power lines leading in.

It would be a long walk in the scorching heat of midday, and he'd better have a drink of the water before he started. He went back and was about to crawl between the strands of barbed wire beside the gate when his attention was suddenly caught by the chain encircling the post. It had been cut.

Somebody had used bolt cutters to remove a quarter-inch section of one side of one of the links, and not too long ago. The clean metallic gray of the ends contrasted sharply with the rusty condition of the rest of it. It had been carefully arranged in back of the post where it would remain unnoticed by anyone going past in front. This had to be the place, he thought, and his eyes were cold as he slipped the adjoining link through the gap and opened the gate.

He could have been the only person in this end of Nevada as he drove through, closed the gate, and rehooked the chain again. There was no dust in sight along the road as far as he could see, no sound of car or truck. As soon as he had dropped down the short grade into the flat, he was out of sight of the road except for the rising dust cloud of his passage. He drove slowly, keeping his eyes on the building for any sign of life. Nothing moved anywhere except the vultures, taking off in alarm as he went past. Whatever carrion they were tearing at was hidden by the sage some hundred yards off to his right.

He was near enough now to see that most of the panes were broken in the old-fashioned sashes of the two windows in front. It was a small house, of board-and-batten construction, long unpainted, with a porch across the front and a roof of weathered shingles. There was a fieldstone chimney at the right end of it. He stopped in the shade of one of the trees in front and got out in the silence and the incandescent glare of noon.

The windmill and the big galvanized water tank were straight ahead, some fifty yards off to the right of the house. Nearly half the mill's blades were missing, and its framework and ladder were discolored with rust. The corral fence and barn were behind the windmill, both silvery with age and fallen into disrepair. It was years, he thought, since anybody had lived here, but the place had definitely had visitors. The baked earth of the yard bore the tracks of at least two vehicles, one of which he thought must have been a truck of some kind because the tires were bigger and the treads more deeply impressed. This one had apparently been back and forth several times.

94

He walked around to the rear. There was a small back porch. The windows here had broken panes in them, too. The tire tracks of the heavy vehicle came on into the back-yard, and the truck or whatever it was had apparently stood for some length of time in two places under the big cotton-wood some distance behind the porch, judging from the ac-cumulated drops of leaking crankcase oil. There were a great many heel marks and scuffs of shoe soles as though a num-ber of people had been walking around, but the ground was too hard-baked and they were too indistinct for him to gather any information from them. The other building, off to one side of the barn, was apparently a chicken house, and there was an old privy farther back.

He walked out to the barn, continuing to study the ground. The wide double doors were open and sagging on their hinges, and the ground was softer inside, a mixture of dust and sand and ancient manure unbaked by the sun. There were some stalls at the far end, an enclosed feed bin, and an opening above leading into a hayloft, but the ladder beneath it was gone except for two rungs near the top. One of the vehicles—the lighter one, he thought—had been driven in here just once and then backed out. A few drops of oil discolored the ground between the tracks where it had stopped, but as a measure of the time it had stood here they were meaningless. One car would drip that much in a few hours, another in a month.

He went back to the rear of the house and stepped up on the porch. The door was closed, but when he tried it, it swung open freely, and he saw it had been forced with a jimmy or pinch bar. It had been a long time ago, however, for there was no raw, fresh look to the splintered wood where the lock had been torn out of the jamb. There was a stovepipe hole and sleeve through the ceiling, so the room had apparently been the kitchen, but nothing remained now except an old table presumably not worth loading when the last occupants moved away. But something was definitely wrong with the picture, and in a moment he realized what it was.

He went on into the room in front, with its fireplace, and then into the remaining two, presumably bedrooms, all empty of any furniture, all with broken windowpanes, and they were the same. There was only the thinnest film of dust, with no footprints visible anywhere. The house had been swept. The floors should have been heavily covered with dust, drifted sand from the broken windows, and probably old rodent droppings and dead insects, but somebody had cleaned it. Why? To remove footprints? And people had been here, presumably for hours or maybe even days, and nowhere had he seen a cigarette butt, an empty cigarette pack, nonreturnable bottle, or tin can. Trespassers with a conscience? Ecology freaks?

He stood in the kitchen again, still puzzled by this, when something shiny caught his eyes in one of the cracks of the floor. When he looked more closely, at different angles, he saw there were several of them. He pulled a thin splinter of wood from the wreckage of the doorjamb and knelt to poke one out. It was smooth, bright, metallic, shaped like a teardrop but flattened on one side. *Solder?* he thought. Here? He lifted out another. There was no doubt of it. They'd fallen into the cracks when the floor was being swept. While there was no electricity for a soldering iron, he knew they were also heated by torches, but what in God's name would somebody have been soldering in this place? He shrugged helplessly and went outside.

There was no litter can or garbage dump anywhere. He went back to the old chicken house and looked inside and behind it. Nothing. He came back and stood under the trees in front, feeling as baffled and frustrated as he had after

96

his interview with Richter. Several people had been here, in two vehicles, they'd cut their way through that chain out there, he was certain this was the place his father had come or been brought at gunpoint; but there wasn't a shred of proof of it or the slightest clue to their identities. Even reporting it to Brubaker was pointless; he wouldn't find anything here either. Of course, he'd probably know who owned the place, but that was of little value. The owners would have entered with a key, not a pair of bolt cutters.

He sighed and got in the car and started back out to the gate. From the sagebrush off to his left, the vultures took off again, flapping clumsily to get themselves aloft. Purely on impulse, he stopped the car and got out. It was probably the carcass of a jackrabbit or a calf, but at least he'd know for sure. As he started out through the brush, he saw a lengthening plume of dust rising from the road. It was coming up from the south, the vehicle itself out of sight beyond the low ridge this side of the gate. He stopped to watch it. It came up to where the gate would be and went past. He went on, beginning to be conscious of the odor of putrefaction. The carcass came into view then. It was a burro, or what was left of one.

It lay in a small open space surrounded by a scattering of greenish-black feathers and the white lime of bird droppings where the vultures had been tearing at it for days or perhaps weeks. All the soft tissues were gone now, consumed by the big birds and the other, smaller scavengers of nature's clean-up crew, so that little remained except the skeleton, some of the tougher connective tissues, and enough of the leathery hide to identify it. He was about to turn back to the car when he noticed a puzzling thing about the skeleton. Nearly all the ribs were broken.

That really was odd, when you thought about it. The scavengers could separate the individual bones as the connective tissues deteriorated, but their breaking anything as strong as the ribs of one of these small desert mules was out of the question. He wondered what could have killed it. The only North American predator with the power to smash in the chest that way would be a grizzly, and there were no grizzlies in the desert or probably anywhere nearer than Yellowstone.

He shrugged. Strange it might be, but not very important. It could have been hit by a car or truck out on the road and then brought in here to be disposed of. He turned away and started back to the car, idly watching the ground for tracks. He'd taken only a few steps when he saw the piece of metal. He picked it up. It was a small aluminum cap, and even as the tingle of excitement began to spread along his nerves, he saw the other thing on the ground—a thin slice of wood veneer the same length as one of the Upmann cigars. It was flat now instead of curled, and somewhat bleached by the sun, but there was no doubt what it was.

What in God's name had the old man been doing out here by the carcass of a burro—assuming the carcass had been here then? And where was the tube itself? He began a search then, slowly, systematically, covering every inch of the ground in a widening spiral outward from the burro. Several times he saw heel prints, but the ground was too hard to tell whether they were all made by the same pair of shoes. The sun beat down relentlessly, and the smell was disagreeable until he began to get farther away. It was obvious now the burro hadn't been dragged in here or unloaded from a truck because no vehicle had been near the place at all, but this interested him only slightly at the moment. It was a full ten minutes before he found anything else, and then it wasn't the cigar tube—he already knew he wasn't going to find that, and why.

It was a small strip of brown plastic or wax-impregnated

cardboard a little more than an inch long and varying from a half inch to an inch in width, jagged of outline and looking as if it had been scorched. It was slightly curved as though it had once been part of a cylinder, and it was crimped at one end. The only images he could evoke from this much of it were of a shotgun shell or a stick of dynamite, but it couldn't be either of these because of the markings. At one end, where it had apparently been crimped, was a plus sign, and at the other, where it was torn and scorched, the two lower-case letters: *fd*. Was there a word in the English language that ended in *fd*? He couldn't think of one, and if he'd ever seen anything resembling this, he couldn't remember it. He put it in the pocket of his shirt.

The three beer cans made even less sense. He found them as he was completing his last circuit, now a good fifty yards away from the burro. They were almost that far again beyond him, toward the house, but sunlight glinting off one of them caught his eye and he went over. They were shiny and new, emptied only recently, and were strung together with short lengths of soft copper wire as if somebody had fashioned a homemade toy for some toddler to drag around. He pulled them from the clump of sage in which they were caught, looked at them blankly, and shook his head.

Their being linked together with the wire seemed too pointless even for speculation, and their only significance was the proof that there had indeed been people here within the past few weeks and that, contrary to the evidence so far, they weren't a new species of man subsisting off the surrounding air in the manner of lichens and orchids, both of which he'd already established when he found the cap to the cigar tube. He tossed them back into the bush, went out to the car, savagely turned it around, and drove back to the house. There were only two possibilities. Either they'd carried everything away with them, in which case he was out

99

of luck, or they'd disposed of it farther from the house, possibly by burning or burying.

He parked in the shade of one of the trees in the rear yard and went straight back, carrying the binoculars. At first the ground was flat, sparsely covered with sage, but after about two hundred yards it rose in a series of low benches, cut here and there by ravines. He climbed up and turned to survey the flat, sweeping the glasses slowly back and forth over all the ground between there and the house. Nothing. He went on, following the course of one of the twisting ravines for several hundred yards, crossed it, and worked his way back down another. The sun was blistering, and sweat ran down his face. Thirst began to bother him, and he wished he'd taken a drink of the water before he started. A jackrabbit burst out of a clump of sage and went bounding off. Heat waves shimmered off the rocky ridge just beyond him to the north. It was a half hour later, and he was a good quarter mile from the house when he found it.

A steep-sided gully about twelve feet deep led off from one of the ravines, and at the bottom of it, half-covered with dead tumbleweeds, were the remains of a fire and a heap of blackened tin cans and broken bottles. He backtracked, found a place to climb down into the ravine, and followed it up to its steep-sided tributary. He entered it, feeling the brutal heat within its constricting walls, and smashed and shoved the old tumbleweeds out of the way.

He found a short piece of stick left over from the fire and began to probe carefully through the pile, separating and cataloging its contents. The labels were all burned off the cans, of course, but at least a dozen of them were food tins—the tops removed completely with a mechanical can opener—in addition to seven fruit-juice tins—punched—and forty-five beer cans. He paused, baffled, as he was tossing the beer cans to one side. Nine of them were tied together with short lengths of copper wire, three in one string and six in another, the same as the ones he'd found out in the flat.

He shrugged and threw them behind him. He could puzzle over that later. There were a number of battered aluminum trays that presumably had held frozen food of some kind, a mustard jar and a pickle jar, both unbroken, and the pieces of what appeared to be two whiskey bottles. Next was a large buckle. It was fire-blackened, and whatever had been attached to it was completely burned away. Then he poked out a short length of stranded copper wire, its insulation burned off. Then another buckle, the same size and shape as the first, and several more scraps of wire, and finally, at the bottom of the whole thing, he began to uncover the cigar tubes he'd been certain he would find. Some of them were flattened and bent and all were scorched by the fire, but there was no doubt they were Upmanns. On a few of them part of the name was still legible. There were twenty-three of them. He tossed the stick aside and stood up.

There was no way of knowing how many people had been here or whether some of the others had been smoking the cigars as well as his father, but even so they could have remained four or five days with the amount of supplies they'd used. They'd obviously had camping equipment, including an icebox and a stove of some kind, and it was possible the heavier vehicle had been a pickup camper. There was little or no chance anybody had seen them while they were in here, since the place was out of sight of the road, but somebody might have seen them coming or going. The thing to do now was report it to Brubaker as soon as possible so he could start questioning the people who used the road. He went back and climbed out of the ravine. Sweat was pouring off his face, and his shirt was stuck to him all over.

He started toward the house but had taken only a few steps when he stopped abruptly, looking out over the flat beyond it. A plume of dust had appeared over the rise just this side of the gate, and the vehicle at the head of it was coming this way in a hurry. He jumped down into the edge of the ravine and lifted the binoculars from their strap around his neck. It was a sports car. It disappeared from view behind the trees before he could get more than this brief glimpse of it, but his eyes were coldly watchful as he waited for it to come into view in the yard at the side of the house. It did in a little more than a minute, and even as it came to a sliding stop, he saw it was Bonner's Porsche.

The big man leaped out, almost before the car had come to a full stop, and lunged toward the wall of the house, flattening himself against it between the windows, and Romstead could see he had the flat slab of an automatic in his hand. He hadn't known the other car was there until he'd made the turn into the yard, Romstead thought. He was being blinded with sweat and had to lower the glasses to wipe it away. When he replaced them, Bonner had eased along the wall until he could peer into the kitchen window.

He went around the corner then, up onto the porch, and pushed the door open and went inside. That took guts, Romstead thought, not knowing who might be in there waiting to blow your head off—guts or wild, bullheaded rage. He'd already seen the other was incongruously dressed in a dark suit, white shirt, and a tie; he'd just come from his sister's funeral.

Bonner emerged from the house, strode to the rented car, and opened the door to lean in. Looking for the registration, Romstead thought. The big man straightened up then with the Steadman County map in his hand. He studied it for a moment, threw it back on the seat, and dropped the automatic in the pocket of his jacket. He strode over to the barn, emerged from that after a brief moment, and went to the chicken house to peer inside. He looked once around the flat and then began to stride furiously straight back toward the hillside and the ravines where Romstead was.

He's not after me, Romstead thought, unless he's gone completely berserk and stopped thinking altogether, but I'd better find out for sure before he gets right on top of me with that gun. Better to have him open up at fifty yards so I can haul ass than to let him stumble over me. He stood up as though he'd just climbed out of the ravine and started to walk toward the other. Bonner saw him but made no move toward the gun in his pocket; he merely quickened his pace. He began to run up the slope toward the bench where Romstead was. When he reached the top he slowed to a furious walk beside the ravine and shouted.

"Romstead! What the hell are you doing here?"

"The same thing you are," Romstead called back.

They were less than twenty yards apart when it happened. Romstead heard the *whuck* of the bullet's slapping into flesh and bone a fraction of a second before he heard the crack of the rifle up on the ridge to his right. Bonner's body jerked with the impact, he spun around, thrown off-balance, and started to fall. There was another *whuck*, and his body jerked again even as it was going down. Romstead was already diving for the ravine. He landed on the sloping side of it and rolled and skidded to the bottom, and as he was spitting out dirt and trying to get the dust and sweat out of his eyes, he heard the rifle fire again.

The ravine was a good seven feet deep, so he was safe here as long as the rifleman stayed where he was, but he had to try to get Bonner down from there if he could locate him. He ran bent over, hugging the wall, and tried to remember just where the big man had fallen. Then he saw the dark coatsleeved arm. The ravine wall was steeper here. He grasped the hand to pull, and at the same time there was another *whuck* above him, followed by the crack of the rifle.

He hauled. Bonner's head and shoulders dangled over the lip of the ravine, and a stream of foamy, bright arterial blood gushed downward through the dust from the throat that was almost completely shot away.

Romstead gagged and retched and pushed himself to one side to get out of the way of it, and then the sickness was gone, and he was conscious only of a cold, consuming rage. He clawed his way up the wall, grasped a protruding root to hold himself there behind the body while he groped in the right-hand pocket of the jacket. He had the automatic then, but it was slick with blood from one of the other wounds, and as he slid back to the bottom of the ravine and started to pull back the slide to arm it, it slipped from his hands. He scooped it up, now pasty with dust, operated the slide, numbly watched the cartridge fly out of the already-loaded chamber, and pounded back up the ravine.

Twenty yards away he threw himself against the sloping wall and inched upward until he could see past a clump of sage at the top. The crest of the ridge ahead of him was at least two hundred and fifty yards away. The handgun, of course, was as useless at that distance as a slingshot, but if the son of a bitch came down to appraise his work and finish off the hiding and unarmed witness, he was going to get the greatest, and last, surprise of his life.

He waited. Minutes crept by. There was no movement anywhere along the ridge. He wiped sweat from his face and left it smeared with blood and dust from his hand. Raising the binoculars, he carefully swept the full crest of the ridge for several hundred yards in both directions and saw nothing but sage and sun-blasted rock. Then he heard a car start up, or a truck, somewhere beyond it. It began to draw away and faded into silence. He turned so he could look out over the flat beyond the ranch house, and in a few minutes he saw the lengthening plume of dust rising from the road as the unseen vehicle sped along it, headed south.

It might be a decoy, he knew; there could have been two of them, one remaining to cut him down when he ventured out into the open, but he didn't think so. A feeling was growing in him now, a totally inexplicable conviction that the rifleman had been up there the whole time he was walking around this hillside and that the man could have killed him fifty times over. Then why Bonner?

In a few minutes he eased back down the ravine to where it shallowed and finally debouched upon the flat. On shaky knees and with his back muscles drawn up into knots, he stepped out into the open and started toward the house. After a hundred yards he began to breathe easily again.

When he got out to the gate, the fence was gone on one side of it. Bonner had apparently just chopped his way through the wire without even looking at the chain. The dust of the other vehicle's passage had long since settled, and there were no others in sight. The wheels spun as he straightened out and gunned it, headed for town.

VIII

"IF you two goddamned bullheaded—" Brubaker searched for a word, gave up in bitter futility, and took a cigar from his desk. He began to strip off the cellophane. "He'd be alive now, but no, he had to go charging out there like a gut-shot rhinoceros instead of telling us about it, whatever it was. And if you can give me one single damned reason on God's green earth why *you* shouldn't be dead too, I'll kiss your ass at half time in the Rose Bowl. Any one of those four slugs he put in Bonner would have killed him, and he could just as easily put the second one in you instead of wasting it on a man who was already as good as dead while he was still falling. Or maybe you're so small he wasn't sure he could hit you at two hundred and fifty yards with probably a twelve power scope, a bench rest, and hand-loaded ammunition that would put all five shots in your eye at that range—"

"I don't know what he was shooting," Romstead said wearily. "All I know is it was plenty hot, and he was an artist with it. And I've already told you, anyway, he could have shot me any time in that half hour I was wandering around there. He must have been up there all the time, and he knew I'd found their garbage dump and those cigar tubes—" He gestured toward the confused litter on Brubaker's desk, the still bloody and dust-smeared automatic, his own statement, now typed out and signed, and half a dozen of the scorched aluminum tubes, a handwritten letter and some more papers, and a flat plastic bag of heroin. "I don't know why he didn't, except it was Bonner he wanted."

It was after 4 P.M. Romstead had returned with them to what he had learned by now was called the old Van Sickle place. Brubaker and another deputy had searched the ridge and the area behind it, found a few footprints and the tracks of a pickup truck or jeep, but no brass. The rifleman had taken his four cartridge cases with him, probably, as Brubaker had said, because they were hand loads instead of factory ammunition, possibly some necked-down and resized wildcat too distinctive to leave lying around. The ambulance had driven out across the flat in back of the house, and they'd carried Bonner's exsanguinated body down from the hillside on a stretcher, looking pitifully shrunken and crumpled in on itself. Romstead had shown them the garbage dump, and after they'd come back to the office, he'd made a full statement and signed it. His face felt sunburned over the old tan and still had dust caked on it. His sweaty clothes had dried now in the air conditioning and stuck to him when he moved.

"Personally," Brubaker said, "I think they set him up with a sucker phone call sometime this morning, because he took off right from his sister's funeral without even going home to change clothes. But now we'll never know. Any more than we'll ever know what he found out in San Francisco or what they were afraid he'd found out. That's the beauty of amateurs showing the police how to do it. By God, *they* don't waste half their time sitting around on their dead asses making out reports like a bunch of dumb cops or even bothering to tell anybody what they're doing." Brubaker removed the cigar from his mouth as if to throw it against the wall but merely cursed again and reclamped it between his teeth.

"Well, he did give you the letter," Romstead said. "When did it come, and specifically what did it say?"

"It came yesterday morning," Brubaker said. "But you might as well read it, since it concerns your old man." He grabbed it out of the confusion on his desk and passed it over.

It was written with a ball-point pen on a single sheet of cheap typing paper. Romstead read it.

Dear Jeri,

   Heres enough for one anyway, its all I can spare the way it is now. But you could easy get that other like I told you on the phone, where I stashed it in the old mans car. For Gods sake dont call here again. If I have to say wrong number one more time hes going to guess who it is and if he even thinks I know where you are he'll beat it out of me and dont think he couldend and wouldent.

                                                        Debra

Romstead sighed and dropped it back on the desk. "So he could, and he did."

Brubaker nodded bleakly. "I'd say so."

"What did the lab report say? Was the stuff cut?"

"Yes. But she still died of an overdose. She probably didn't shoot it herself, though."

"No," Romstead said. "Of course not. If the stuff was in the car, probably behind the seat cushions somewhere, the dresser was a phony. And in that case, so was the whole thing. They were waiting for her out there—or *he* was, whoever the hell he is—knowing an addict would eventually show up where the junk was. Did you get the phone number?"

"We occasionally think of things like that," Brubaker said wearily. He picked up another sheet of paper. "She came home on Tuesday of last week, apparently with enough of the stuff to keep her going for a few days, but by Monday she was climbing into the light fixtures. Monday evening, after Bonner'd gone to work, there were five toll calls to this number in San Francisco at twenty to thirty-minute intervals. Maybe sometimes the man would answer and she'd just hang up, or Debra would answer but he was still home, so she'd say wrong number. This, so help me God, to the home phone of a man who's apparently trying to find her so he can kill her. Junk." He shook his head and went on. "Anyway, she and Debra must have made connections on the fifth call, and Debra told her about the deck she'd hidden in your father's car and maybe promised to send her enough for a fix if she could.

"I guess Jeri didn't think that night she knew how to break into a house, but another thirty hours of withdrawal symptoms and she didn't have any doubt of it at all. She could break into Fort Knox with a banana. So she went out there sometime after two o'clock Wednesday morning, as soon as Bonner was asleep. And in the meantime, apparently Debra'd been worked over till she broke down and told the man about it, so he was waiting. Obviously he didn't guess about the letter, though.

"The San Francisco police got the name and address from the phone company. J. L. Stacey, probably an alias, in a furnished apartment out near North Beach, but when they got there, the birds were gone without a trace. Bonner, of course, couldn't have got the information, so I guess he was just going it blind, trying to run down somebody who knew who Debra was.

"And, incidentally, while we're on the subject of phone calls, both of those your father made"—Brubaker picked up another sheet of paper from the litter on his desk—"to Winegaard at seven A.M. July sixth and to Richter at ten fifteen A.M. July tenth, were from his home phone. So whatever he was doing out there at the Van Sickle place, he came home on Monday to phone and then left again, for God knows where until he showed up at the bank on the morning of the twelfth."

"He didn't *go* anywhere, from beginning to end," Romstead said. "He was taken. He was kidnapped."

Brubaker got up and began to pace the office. "Jesus Christ, when I think that I could've been a pimp or a geek in a sideshow, biting the heads off chickens! Look, Romstead, kidnap is a federal offense, and if we had one single damned shred of evidence to hang a kidnap case on, we could call in the FBI. We'd have a whole army of special agents working on it. As a matter of fact, I've talked to them, but after they talked to Richter, they said forget it. They must have thought I was nuts. And Richter, believe me, is getting plenty pissed about it. He says he's going to make a recording. First there was Sam Bolling, and then the San Francisco police, and then you, and then the FBI, and then me.

"So maybe I was wrong about the heroin theory, so I don't have the faintest damned idea what he was doing out there at the old Van Sickle place or what he did with that two hundred and fifty thousand dollars, there is no evidence whatever he was there, or anywhere else, against his will, and how in hell"—Brubaker dropped into his chair again and slammed a hand down on his desk among the papers—"how in hell—you tell me—could he have been kidnapped if he came into that bank himself—alone—to get the money?"

"I don't know," Romstead replied. "But I'm going to find out." He got up.

"Well, there's no way I can stop you from trying. But did you ever hear the old story about the man tracking the tiger through the jungle?"

Romstead nodded. "Yeah, I know."

"Well, if I were you I'd keep a good lookout behind. That second set of tiger tracks may be closer than you think."

He went back to the motel and called Mayo. She grabbed up the phone on the first ring, and he gave a sigh of relief as he heard her voice.

"I've been worried all day," she said.

"Not too worried to go out with another man. I tried to call you around eleven."

"Oh, hell, of all the rotten luck. That's when I ducked downstairs to get the mail. And I wasn't gone five minutes. Did you find the place?"

"Yes. But there's nobody there now and nothing to prove who they were." He had no intention of saying anything about Bonner. "I'll tell you about it when I get there. I'm not sure yet what flight I'll be on, so don't figure on meeting me at the airport. Just stay near the phone, and I'll call as soon as I'm in town. Should be before ten."

"Are you leaving for Reno now?"

"Very shortly. Just as soon as I talk to Mrs. Carmody."

"Hah! Maybe *she's* the reason I couldn't come with you."

"You're obsessed with sex. You ought to see somebody about it."

"Maybe I would, if you ever got home. But while you're visiting your father's sexpot, keep reminding yourself of the Oedipal overtones."

"Hell, just thinking of the comparisons would do it."

"That'll be the day."

After he'd hung up, he debated whether to put through a call to Murdock. No, that could wait till he'd talked to Paulette Carmody; he'd call after he was back in San Francisco. He showered and put on a fresh shirt and a tie and the suit he'd worn coming up. As he was putting the dusty and sweat-stained shirt in the bag, he remembered the fragment of brown plastic or cardboard he'd found out in the flat by the dead burro. He removed it from the pocket.

What could *fd* mean? *Mfd* for manufactured? No, there'd have to be something after it. *Mfd by,* or *Mfd in—* He frowned. Solder. Radio officer. *Check out the simalizer and put a new frammistat in his KLH.* Jeri Bonner had worked for an electronics supply company, probably where she'd met Tallant. He grabbed up the telephone directory and flipped through the thin section of yellow pages. RADIO AND TV, REPAIRS. There were three, one of them on West Third Street. Well, they couldn't lock you up for asking stupid questions. He dropped it in the pocket of his jacket and finished packing.

He carried the bag out to the car and stopped at the office to pay for the toll calls and the extra day. The sour-faced man was behind the desk.

"Have to pay for an extra day," he said. "Checkout time's two P.M. Same's it has been for years."

"Right." Romstead put down the Amex card.

"You'd think someday people'd learn—"

Romstead picked up the card and put down two twenty-dollar bills. It'd be quicker, and he wouldn't have to listen to the old fart.

"Posted right there on the wall, plain as anything."

Romstead picked up the change, his face suffused with wonder. "Well, I be dawg; so that's what that writin' said? I thought it meant I could take the towels for keepsakes."

He went up Aspen and made the turn into Third. The TV repair shop was near the end of the block with a parking space a few doors away. It was after five now, and he hoped it wasn't closed. It wasn't, quite. At the counter in front a girl was putting on lipstick and appraising her hair in a small mirror. In back of her was an open doorway into the shop.

"Are any of your service men still here?" he asked her.

"Yes," she said. "Raymond's back there. We're about to close, though."

"This'll only take a minute." He went around the end of the counter. There were two service benches in the back room with long fluorescent lights above them, littered with tools and parts and the denuded carcasses of TV sets and radios. Raymond was a pleasant long-haired youth wearing a University of Nevada T-shirt. He glanced up inquiringly from the writhing green snakes he was watching on the screen of some kind of test equipment.

"I just wanted to ask you what may be a very dumb question." Romstead set the fragment of plastic on the bench. "Is this part of anything electronic?"

Raymond glanced at it, turned it slightly to look at the markings. "Sure," he said. He reached into a bin and brought out a cylindrical object that reminded Romstead vaguely of a shotgun shell except that it had a short piece of wire attached to each end. He set it on the bench. It was imprinted with the manufacturer's name, but what instantly caught Romstead's eye was the legend, "100 Mfd," in the center of it. There was a minus sign at one end and a plus at the other.

"Electrolytic capacitor," Raymond said. " 'Mfd' is the abbreviation for microfarad. They're used in a number of different circuits for high capacity at a low-voltage rating. Have to be installed with the right polarity, though; that's the reason for the plus and minus on the case."

Romstead understood little or nothing of this except that his stab in the dark had paid off. He smiled at Raymond and put five dollars on the bench. "Thanks a million," he said. "I won the bet."

He drove on out West Third Street in the sunset, wondering if he hadn't merely made the whole thing worse; certainly you could go crazy trying to figure out what all these different parts had to do with each other or with his father's inexplicable trip to the bank. Lost in thought, he almost went past Paulette Carmody's drive and had to slam on his brakes to make the turn. He parked in front of the walk on the circular blacktop drive and went up to ring the bell, thinking now that it was too late, that he should have called first. She'd probably heard about Bonner by now and might not feel like talking to anybody. She came to the door herself, and he suspected she'd been crying, though she'd done a good job of covering the effects with makeup. He started to apologize, but she interrupted.

"No," she said. "I'm glad you came; I wanted to talk to you." She led the way down the short vestibule into the living room. "Come on into the kitchen," she said, "while I fix the drinks. It's Carmelita's day off."

The kitchen was in front, on the opposite side of the living room, with a separate dining room in back of it. There was a door at the far end of it, probably to the garage. She opened the refrigerator for ice cubes. "Martini, vodka and tonic, scotch?"

"Vodka and tonic would be fine," he said.

She began assembling the drinks, the old ebullience and blatant sexiness subdued now, though the simple sheath she wore was still overpowered by the figure that nothing would ever quite restrain. Her legs were bare, as usual.

"I'm sorry about Bonner," he said.

"He made a lot of enemies," she replied, "but I liked him. He was hard-nosed, bullheaded, and horny, and always in a brawl or trouble of some kind, but in most ways he was a simplehearted and generous kind of guy and a good friend. And lousy husband, naturally."

"Then he'd been married?"

114

"Oh, yes, for about six years. But his wife finally gave up. Poker, and cheating on her all the time. Men. I'll swear to Christ."

They carried their drinks into the living room. Dusk was thickening in the patio beyond the wall of glass, and the pool was a shimmering blue with its underwater lights. She had heard very little of how it had happened, so he told her, playing down the gory aspects of it as much as possible.

"Then Brubaker thinks Jeri was killed, too?" she asked. "And Lew had an idea who did it?"

"Or at least they were afraid he did."

"You realize you could have been shot, too?"

"I guess he wasn't worried about me," Romstead replied. That was no answer, he knew, but he didn't have any better. "But about that radio officer on the *Fairisle*, was his name Tallant?"

"No," she said. "Kessler. Harry Kessler."

That wasn't conclusive, Romstead thought; he could have changed it, unless he was on parole. "You knew him about four years ago?"

"That's right. Actually, it was five years ago, of course, when your father picked us up out there, but I hardly noticed him then. Jeri did, though. She thought he was cute."

"He'd have been in his late twenties? Medium height, slender, dark complexion, brown eyes, black hair?"

"Oh, no. The age and the build would be about right, but he was as blond as you are. Blue eyes."

Romstead glumly shook his head. So much for that brainstorm. But then how did Tallant get into the picture?

"Anyway," Paulette went on, "it seems to me he'd still be in prison. I don't know how long a sentence he got, but it's only been a little over three years."

"Do you know where he was sent?"

She shook her head. "No, except that it must have been

115

a federal prison. This happened at sea, so I don't think any state would have had jurisdiction."

"How'd the old man get wise to him anyway?"

She set her drink on the coffee table and lighted a cigarette. "Your father could read code, and Kessler didn't know it. You see, when he was a young man and still sailing as mate on Norwegian ships—"

"Yes, I know about that," Romstead interrupted. "He used to have both licenses and doubled as radio operator sometimes. Winegaard told me about it."

"That's right. And I gather that reading code is something you never entirely forget. You may get a little rusty, but you can always do it, like swimming or riding a bicycle. But I'd better start at the beginning.

"It was in 1968, when I made the first trip as passenger on the *Fairisle*, that I got to know this kook. I guess from what everybody said he was close to being an authentic genius—in electronics, anyway—but he didn't have an engineering degree for some reason; maybe he'd been too poor to go to college or he'd been kicked out or something. Otherwise, he'd probably have been drawing a big salary in one of those fur-brain outfits doing research and making Buck Rogers stuff for satellites and moon shots and so on. He was always inventing things and experimenting and lashing up nutty pieces of electronic spaghetti so he could stare into the screen of an oscilloscope like somebody watching a dirty movie, and the radio room looked like a mad scientist's nightmare. There was no doubt he had a brilliant mind; but he could be pretty contemptuous and snotty, and he had a sadistic sense of humor. I didn't much like him, though he could be charming when he wanted to be.

"Anyway, at the end of the next trip, when I met your father in San Francisco, he said he was going to be tied up part of the time making depositions and affidavits and so on, and it turns out it was about this screwball Kessler. He told me what had happened. Maybe I should have told you first that for two or three trips the Customs men had really been shaking down the *Fairisle* when she came in from the Far East, going over her with a fine-tooth comb as if they'd had a tip there was contraband aboard, but they never found anything.

"Well, this trip, about ten P.M. the last night out from San Francisco, your father was down in the passengers' lounge playing bridge. There was a radio in the lounge, turned on and getting music from some station ashore, and all of a sudden the music began to be covered up with dots and dashes —code, that is. Your father explained to me why it was. It seems if a transmitter's antenna and a receiver's antenna are right close together, the way they'd be aboard a ship, the receiver would pick up what was being sent by the transmitter even though they might be tuned to different wavelengths. It sort of spills over into it or something.

"It was perfectly normal, of course, and happened every time Kessler was using the ship's transmitting apparatus, but your father began reading it just automatically while he went on playing bridge, and in a minute he realized there was something damned screwy about what Kessler was sending. It wasn't any message *he'd* given him to send, in the first place, and he wasn't using any of the standard procedure or the ship's call letters or identification of any kind. But it was a sort of ETA—estimated time of arrival—only it wasn't seven A.M., when the *Fairisle* was due to arrive off the Golden Gate, but four A.M., when she'd still be over fifty miles at sea. So it had to be a rendezvous with a boat of some kind.

"Your father said nothing about it to the passengers, of course, and went ahead and finished the card game. When he went back up to his cabin, he phoned the bridge and

117

left orders to be called at three A.M. He went up to the bridge at that time and switched on the radar. There were three or four ships showing on the screen, and in a few minutes he began to pick up another, much smaller target, which was probably a small boat. It was ahead of the *Fairisle*, more or less stationary, and he could see they were going to pass it less than a mile off.

"He went down and woke up the chief officer. He wanted a witness, for one thing, and the chief officer's cabin was in the same passageway as Kessler's. They watched with the door on a crack, and in a few minutes Kessler looked out of his cabin to be sure the coast was clear and then started down the passageway toward the deck, carrying what looked like just a bunch of junk he wanted to heave over the side.

"Your father stepped out and collared him. Kessler began cursing and trying to fight him off, so your father slugged him. He had a fist like a twelve pound frozen ham, so Kessler'd had all the fight knocked out of him by the time he was able to stand up again. Your father had him locked up, and he and the chief officer checked over this thing he'd been carrying. It was a big jagged piece of styrofoam that'd been stained brown so it'd look like an old chunk of wood. There was a thin wire sticking up through it and the thing was ballasted on the bottom so the wire would stay upright. Inside the styrofoam was a real tiny radio transmitter—it turned out to be when the narcs got hold of it—using the wire for an antenna. And attached to the bottom with stainless-steel wire was a watertight plastic container with nearly a half kilo of heroin in it.

"Well, Kessler never would identify the people on the boat, but he did cop out to the extent of explaining how it worked, which the narcs knew anyway. He'd built the little transmitter, of course, and on the boat there was a small radio direction-finder he'd also built. It was tuned to the same frequency as the transmitter, so all the boat people had to do was home in on the signal until they could pick up the float in their searchlight. They'd pulled it off twice before and got away with it.

"Your father had to take part of a trip off to testify at the trial, about ten months later, I think. He left the ship in San Francisco and rejoined it in Honolulu. Kessler was convicted, but I never did know what sentence he got."

Paulette fell silent and took a sip of her drink.

"He didn't make any threats of any kind against the old man?" Romstead asked.

She shook her head. "Not that I know of."

Revenge could have been a motive, of course, along with the quarter million dollars, and he was thinking of that lactose poured in his father's mouth, in conjunction with another thing she'd said.

"You said he had a sadistic sense of humor. How was that?"

"Oh, nutty practical jokes, things like that, with the electronics junk he was always experimenting with. Real tiny bugging devices almost as far out as the old gag about the bugged martini olive. Wiring a girl's room in a cathouse was a big laugh. And then the creepy things he remote-controlled by radio—"

"Remote control?" Romstead interrupted. He frowned.

"Sure, you know. Like those model airplanes people fly with little transmitters that make 'em bank and turn and loop-the-loop. Of course, he didn't invent the idea; it's been around for years, but he added his own touches. He was a little hipped on the whole subject, as a matter of fact, and used to brag he could radio-control anything if you paid him enough.

"For example, he bought a couple of battery-operated toy cars and tore them down and rebuilt them with radio controls for starting and stopping and turning. Then he paid a kid in Manila to kill him two of those big gruesome rats on the docks there—I mean, they're something else. Any tomcat crazy enough to tackle one of 'em, I'd give you the tomcat and eight points. He tanned the skins and built foam-rubber bodies for the cars and sewed the skins over them. Talk about freezing your blood, to see those two things coming at you in formation. He used to take them ashore with him; they say he could empty a whorehouse in ten seconds."

Romstead felt the hair stabbing the back of his neck. His mind was racing now as all the bits and pieces began to fall into place. He thought of the terrified little burro fleeing out across the flat with its clattering beer cans, and then exploding. . . . "The subhuman son of a bitch," he said.

He hadn't realized he'd spoken aloud until Paulette looked at him blankly and said, "What?"

"Don't you see? That's what nobody's ever been able to figure out—how the old man could be forced to go into the bank alone and cash that check. You've just told me."

"Eric, darling," she said, "you're farther around the bend than Kessler. You don't remote-control a man, and certainly not that one."

"Oh, yes, you can," he replied, "if the threat is right. Tell me, didn't Kessler wear glasses?"

"Yes. He was myopic, I think. How'd you guess?"

"The color of his eyes has changed. He's wearing tinted contacts." Dyeing the hair was routine, of course, and there were drugs that would darken the skin. He must be out on parole, so he'd violated it and skipped from wherever he was supposed to be, which meant he'd been up to something criminal all along. He'd run into Jeri at that electronics supply place where she worked, and even if she hadn't recognized him, he remembered her—

Romstead's thoughts broke off as he realized Paulette was asking him something over and over.

"Eric, for God's sake, what do you *mean*, if the threat is right?"

"A radio-detonated explosive device on him somewhere, probably in the crotch. Having somebody by the balls is not just an expression."

"But why couldn't he tell somebody?"

"You just told me that too. He was bugged. Whatever he said to anybody or anybody said to him was being piped right into the ear of the bastard with the control transmitter. Kessler. Got up as a hippie with hair down to his shoulders to hide the plug in his ear. I've got to call Brubaker."

The chief deputy might be home by now, but he could try the office first. He flipped the directory open to the emergency numbers and picked up the receiver. Before he could start to dial, the tone went off. He jiggled the switch. Nothing.

"Your phone's gone dead," he said.

Paulette Carmody looked up in surprise. "That's funny. It was all right a half hour ago." She put down her drink. "I'll try the bedroom extension."

She went through the foyer toward the bedroom wing and came back in a moment, shaking her head. "Dead as Kelsey's jewels."

The lights went out all over the house, and then those in the pool. The faint humming of the air conditioner stopped. In blackness and total silence he thought he heard a door open somewhere and at the same time the sharp indrawn breath of an incipient outcry from Paulette. He reached for her, got a hand over her mouth, and pushed her down to the floor beside the sofa.

IX

HE placed his lips against her ear and whispered, "Stay down." Feeling her head move as she nodded, he pushed away from her and stood up, trying to remember the dimensions of the room and the placement of all its furniture. He didn't know which door it was he'd heard, but it was most likely the one at the other end of the kitchen; the electric panel with its switches and circuit breakers would probably be in the garage.

His eyes hadn't had time to adjust yet, and the blackness was still impenetrable as he began to feel his way toward the wall by the kitchen doorway. He stopped to listen. He was on carpet, but if somebody were traversing the tile floor of the kitchen he should make some sound. The silence was unbroken. He stepped forward again, his hands groping for contact with the wall. Then the light burst in his face. Paulette screamed behind him.

It was white, focused, and blinding for an instant, the beam of a six-cell flashlight, and just below it and extending slightly into the beam were the ugly twin tubes of a sawed-off shotgun. He froze where he was, a good six feet from the ends of the barrels, and he could make out a little of the shadowy form behind the light. The man was clad in a black jump suit and black hangman's hood. He'd made no sound on the kitchen floor because he was wearing only socks. They were black, too. Paulette screamed again. There must be another one behind him.

"Well," the man with the shotgun said, "if you want to carry the big son of a bitch—"

Romstead started to turn his head. A fiery blossom of pain exploded inside it. The light in front of his eyes receded to some great distance and then went out.

He opened his eyes, winced, and closed them again as he fought off waves of nausea. In a moment he tried once more. It appeared to be daylight wherever he was—faint daylight, to be sure, but at least he could see. He was lying fully clothed except for coat and tie on a narrow and too-short bed covered with a blue chenille spread, looking up at what appeared to be a varnished knotty-pine ceiling. He was a light drinker, and only a very few times in his life had he consumed enough to have a hangover; but he was conscious of some woolly and unfocused impression that this must be the distilled essence of all the hangovers in history. His mind was beginning to function a little now, however, and he remembered the man with the shotgun and Paulette Carmody's warning cry. He put a hand up to his head. There was a painful lump at the back of it, and his hair was matted with dried blood.

He looked at his watch. When he could get the face of it to swim into focus he saw it was ten minutes of nine. A.M.? he wondered. But it had to be; it was daylight. How in hell could he have been unconscious for—what was it—fifteen hours?

He gave up on that and turned his head, accepting the stab of pain he knew this was going to cost. Just beyond him was another narrow bed, the other of the set of twins and similarly covered with a blue chenille spread. Paulette Carmody lay on it, asleep, blond hair tousled and the wrinkled dress halfway up her thighs. Beyond her, at the end of a room which appeared to be all varnished pine, was the window from which the light was coming, what there was of it. It was barred. A small air conditioner was set in the bottom of it, and outside it the louvered shutters were closed.

Barred? He turned his head to the right. There was a door at that end of the room, armored with a thin plate of steel bolted at all four corners. Just to the right of it were two chests of drawers set side by side. Atop one of them was an intercom, and above the other a wall-mounted mirror and what looked like a sliding panel or pass-through below it. The panel was closed. But there was another door in the wall opposite the foot of the bed. It was ajar.

He swung his feet to the floor and sat up. Pain clamped its viselike grip on his head again, and he was assailed by vertigo. He tried to stand but fell back on the side of the bed. There was no feeling in his feet at all and no control over the muscles in his ankles. Apparently he'd been lying for a long time with his feet extending over the end of the bed, their own weight and that of the heavy brogues cutting off most of the circulation. He leaned down, managed to worry the shoes off, and began to massage them. They were swollen and as devoid of sensation as blocks of wood at first, but in a minute he could feel the pinpricks of returning circulation.

He could stand now. He swayed once and then lurched drunkenly over to the door that was ajar. It was a bathroom. There was a small window at the back of it, but it was covered with two vertical strips of two-by-two angle iron bolted at top and bottom. He stared at it numbly for a moment and then went over to the steel-faced door at the front of the room. He tried the knob. It was locked. And probably bolted on the outside, too, he thought. There was a faint humming sound from the air conditioner in the other window, but otherwise, the silence was total.

He went back to the window and examined it. They weren't bars, as he'd thought at first, but lengths of two-by-two angle iron the same as those across the bathroom window. Only here, in order to clear the air-conditioner controls, they'd bolted horizontal lengths to the wall at top and bottom and then welded three vertical strips to them. The bolts were half-inch, he thought, the steel was quarter-inch stock, and the welds looked solid. He caught one of the vertical strips, put a foot against the wall, and heaved back. Nothing happened except that it made his head pound. You couldn't budge it with a crowbar, he thought.

He held a hand in front of the air-conditioner grille. It was only the fan that was turned on, for ventilation. He put his face between two of the vertical angle irons, as near the window as he could get, and looked downward with the slope of the louvers outside. At first all he saw was the top of the external portion of the air conditioner. There was sunlight on it. The surface was weather-stained, and he could see dust on it and several pine needles. He moved over to the edge of the window, looked slantingly downward past the air-conditioner box, and saw a few feet of stony ground, the half-exposed root of a tree, and more pine needles.

Wherever they were, he thought, it wasn't in the desert. Pines didn't grow there, at least not at low altitudes. He turned back to the room. When Paulette Carmody woke up, maybe she could tell him what had happened and where they were. They surely hadn't slugged her, too. She had turned again in her sleep, and the dress was now up around her hips. He pulled the spread off the other bed and covered her legs with it. She was going to have enough to cope with when she woke up, without being embarrassed on top of it.

He went back into the bathroom. The floor was badly worn linoleum but seemed to be clean. There was a commode and a washbasin with rust streaks under the spigots. Above the basin was a cloudy mirror. An old-fashioned tub with claw feet stood in a rear corner next to the window. There was a louvered shutter outside the window, the same as the one in the bedroom, so it was scarcely twilight inside the room. He flicked a switch, and a light came on above the mirror. A rack held a supply of towels, and there was a wrapped bar of soap on the side of the basin. He turned on the cold-water tap and washed his face. It made him feel a little better. The water was icy, which seemed further evidence they must be in the Sierra or at least in the foothills. And the place must be completely isolated, far from any traveled road. He hadn't heard a car yet.

But how could he have been unconscious for that long? He'd been knocked out several times in his life but never for more than a few minutes, and he'd never heard of fifteen hours or longer except in cases of severe concussion and coma. He must have been drugged with something. His coat had been removed, and his tie, and he noticed now that the cuff of his left shirt sleeve was unbuttoned. He pulled the sleeve up and saw them immediately, two small blue puncture marks and a drop of dried blood. They'd used the tie for a tourniquet. And some junkie's dirty needle, he thought, and then wondered if he were entirely rational even yet if he didn't have any more to worry about under the circumstances than serum hepatitis.

He pulled open the mirrored door of the medicine cabinet. Inside were two new toothbrushes in plastic tubes, some toothpaste, a bottle of aspirin, and a water tumbler. He shook out four of the aspirin and examined them. They bore the well-known brand name and appeared to be genuine. He swallowed them, broke open one of the toothbrushes, and scrubbed vigorously at his teeth.

He came back out into the room. A curtained alcove to

126

the left of the bathroom proved to be a closet. Several wire coat hangers dangled from a rod, and his suitcase, Paulette Carmody's handbag, and a small overnight case were on the floor. His coat and tie were tossed across his bag. He let the curtain fall back into place and went over to the two chests of drawers against the front wall.

The intercom would be open, of course, and no doubt there was another bug somewhere in the room, or perhaps two, so after they'd muffled the intercom with a pillow and found the obvious bug, the plant, and pulled its teeth, there'd still be another recording everything they said. The mirror was obviously phony; on the other side of its dark and imperfect reflection it was a window through which they could be watched as long as the light intensity was higher on this side than on the other. He looked up. In the ceiling was a light fixture with what appeared to be a 200-watt bulb in it. It wasn't turned on at the moment, but it would be at night. He could smash it, of course, but to what point? The spooks would simply come in with that sawed-off shotgun and tie them up.

Did the crazy bastard think he could get away with it again? It was obvious, now that it was too late, what Kessler had been looking for in his apartment; he'd even told Mayo, without realizing it. Bank statements. The hundred and seventy-two thousand dollars on deposit at the Southland Trust in San Diego, everything he had in the world except for the few hundred in the checking account in San Francisco. And now he was being programmed to go in and draw it out with a fatal third testicle of plastic explosive in a jockstrap or a stick of dynamite taped to the inside of his leg. This would be inside three or four pairs of panty hose, probably sewn to the bottom of a T-shirt, and finally covered by trousers with the belt and fly zipper jammed in some way. In ten minutes you could work your way out of it, and in one second or less you could be mutilated and dying. But what about the radio circuits and the other wires connecting them to the detonator? They must have been inside the old man's coat somewhere, so why hadn't he been able to get at them and disable the apparatus? His hands had been free. No doubt he'd find out, but at the moment there appeared to be no answer except that you never made any sudden and impulsive moves when somebody had you by the jewels.

But why had they kidnapped Paulette Carmody? Why, for that matter, had they gone to the trouble to bug her telephone and then close in on him while he was at her place? There didn't seem to be any answer to these questions either. Then, for the first time, the absolute silence of the place was broken; from the other side of the wall against which the beds were placed there came a low murmur of voices and the creaking of a bed. He turned and looked at Paulette Carmody. Her eyes were open. She stared blankly at him for a moment and then put a hand up to her head, and said, "Good God!"

"They didn't slug you too, did they?" he asked.

"No," she said. "It must be that crap they shot into my arm. Battery solution or varnish remover."

"I'm sorry about it," he said.

"About what?"

"Getting you involved. I don't know why they grabbed you too."

"Money," she said. She sat up with a grimace of pain and grabbed her head again, felt the disarray of her hair, and shuddered. He wanted to ask her what money and how they expected to get it, but it could wait. He brought her purse and the small overnight case from the closet and set them beside her. "There's a bathroom," he said. "And a toothbrush and some aspirin. Can you make it?"

She nodded. She pushed aside the bedspread he'd put over

128

her, swung bare legs off the bed, and stood up. When she swayed drunkenly, he took her by the arm and helped her to the door of the bathroom and then passed in her purse. The creaking of the bed in the other room was increasing now, and he could hear the voices again. One of them was feminine. There began a series of little moans and gasping outcries. He cursed and hoped they'd get it over with before Paulette came out of the bathroom. They didn't. When she emerged a few minutes later, wearing lipstick now and still running a comb through her hair, she walked right into it. There was a sudden crescendo of the lunging of the bed, its headboard banging against a wall apparently as sound-transparent as paper, and then a ragged and strangely hoarse but unmistakably feminine voice cried out, "Now, now, now! Oh, Jesus Christ, oh, God!" They looked away from each other in embarrassment as this ended in one final chaotic shriek and silence descended.

Paulette sat on the side of the bed and fished a cigarette out of her purse. "Well, at least they didn't put it on closed-circuit TV and make us watch. Though I wouldn't put it past the creepy dingaling."

He gestured toward the intercom. "The room's bugged."

"So let him listen. What difference does it make?" she asked.

"None, now." If her telephone had been tapped, Kessler already knew they had figured out his identity and they were doomed from the start, in spite of the window dressing of the hoods and masks.

"It's my fault," he said. "I blew it from every angle. If I hadn't shot off my mouth—"

"Will you stop it? None of it is your fault. I was the primary target all along. From the little I overheard, you're just going to pick up the ransom."

"How much?"

129

"Two million."

He whistled. "How do they expect to get it?"

"I don't know. They didn't discuss it much, except one of them suggested they avail themselves of the facilities while they had me there alone with you drugged and knocked out. The other one told him to shut up and attend to business. That's when the two million was mentioned. You could be swimming in it, he said, in that bracket. Wall-to-wall tail is the elegant way he put it."

"Then there were just two of them?"

"That's all I saw."

"Was one of them Kessler? Or would you be able to recognize his voice?"

"I might. But they were both too big, six feet or over. One had a hush-puppy accent, Texas, I think."

"So there are three of them, at least."

She gestured toward the wall. "Plus Hotpants."

"Did you get a look at their car?"

"No. I think it must have been down the hill in back, at your father's place. After they slugged you and injected that stuff in your arm, they held me and gave me a shot of it, too. Then the one who seemed to be in charge sent Tex off to get the wheels. Tex was the one who was smitten by my desirability. Or maybe availability is the word. Anyway, the stuff didn't take effect right away, and I was still with it to some extent when I heard the car pull up in front; but by the time they'd lugged you out there and then come back for me I was out. I have some kind of vague impression of about halfway waking up somewhere along the line and the two of us were lying on a mattress in the back of what might have been a panel truck. We were stopped, and they seemed to be giving you the needle again. But the whole thing might have been a dream."

"No. There are two punctures."

"But why the drugs at all? They could have just tied us up."

"So we wouldn't be able even to make a guess which direction we were driven or for how long. We could be twenty miles west of Coleville or four hundred miles south. I think we're in the Sierra or the foothills, for what that's worth, which is nothing."

"Do you suppose they're going to do the same thing again, send you into the bank for the money the way they did your father?"

"Apparently. It worked the other time, so maybe they think they can get away with it again."

"But there's one thing I still don't understand. His hands were free, of course, so why couldn't he—"

"Time," he said. He explained. "He'd have been blown up before he could even start to get out of it."

"But, Eric, part of the junk must have been somewhere else on him. In his coat, maybe, so there'd have to be interconnection wires he could yank loose."

"Yeah, I know—" he began, but at that moment the intercom came to life.

"Of course he could have pulled the circuits apart," a voice said. "But that was the last thing on earth he wanted. Believe me."

They looked at each other. The question was obvious in Romstead's eyes. She shrugged. It could be Kessler, but she wasn't sure.

Romstead turned toward the intercom. "Why?"

"You know anything about electrical circuits or electronics?" the voice asked.

"Very little," Romstead said bleakly.

"Well, your old man did. He got it right away when I showed him the circuit."

"You want me to ask, is that it?"

"I don't care if you do or not, but I think you ought to understand what you're up against. The detonator was on the back contact of the relay. Fail-safe in reverse."

"All right, whatever that means."

"It means, quite simply, that the thing wasn't intended to be detonated by the radio signal. It was the radio signal that kept it *from* detonating, if you're still with me. He was on a leash."

Romstead got it then, the full horror of it and the helplessness his father must have felt. He couldn't run, because if he went beyond the range of the transmitter he'd blow up automatically. If the police grabbed Kessler, or if he himself got close enough to grab him or knock him out, the same thing would happen.

"The spark supply was self-contained," the voice went on. "A bank of charged capacitors. Perfectly harmless as long as the detonating circuit was open, but if the radio circuit failed for any reason, the relay fell open and completed the detonating circuit through the back contact. Neat device."

Egomaniac, Romstead thought. He was capable of talking himself into the gas chamber just to prove how brilliant he was. But that was of little help here.

"Now we're all agreed you're a genius," Romstead said, "do we have to have the burro?"

"No, we haven't got another burro. We've got some good sixteen millimeter footage of that one, though, if you need convincing."

Romstead said nothing. The bed was beginning to creak again on the other side of the wall. The voice went on, "Not necessary, anyway. You don't think we're stupid enough to try the same thing again in the same way, do you? This is a whole new operation with a different approach. Do you want some breakfast?"

"Oh, God," the girl said on the other side of the wall. Romstead looked at Paulette Carmody. She shook her head and looked away.

"We appreciate it," Romstead said, "but not with the present entertainment."

There was a chuckle from the intercom. "Boy, have you got hangups. Well, we're going to bring you out in a little while for the pictures we have to have."

The headboard of the other bed was beginning to bump the wall once more. "Fast turnaround; no down time at all," Paulette Carmody said. "Or she's taking them in relays." She went into the bathroom and closed the door. He heard her flush the toilet and turn on the water in the basin. After the final shriek she came out again.

"And I always loved sex," she said. "Do you suppose I'll ever be capable of it again?"

"Sure," Romstead replied. "Barnyard matings never bothered you before, did they?"

She lighted another cigarette. "It's a wonder the great genius didn't put a TV camera in here so they could watch us as well as listen."

"Oh, we're being watched." He gestured toward the front wall. "The mirror's a phony."

She looked at it with interest. "You mean like those they're supposed to have in some of the casinos? How does it work?"

"You just have to have more light on the front side than the back. It's probably in a closet out there, or there's a curtain over it."

"Oh. What was all that about a burro?"

He explained about finding the skeleton with its broken ribs. "It was a demonstration, to put the old man in a receptive frame of mind. They strapped a bundle of dynamite to the poor little bastard, tied some tin cans to his tail to make him run, and then blew him up several hundred yards away."

"Oh, my God! How sick can you get? And they took movies of it?"

"So he says."

"But how could they get them developed?"

"Some bootleg lab that does processing for stag movies."

She gave him a speculative glance. "For an ex-jock and a prosaic businessman, you seem to know some of the damndest things."

He shrugged. "I read a lot."

"Yes, but I wonder what."

He made no reply. Two million dollars, she'd said; he'd had no idea she was that wealthy, but Kessler must have, and apparently he was right. His intelligence operations must have improved since they'd kidnapped his father. He thought of Jeri; maybe that had been her job and she'd bungled it. But how in hell did they expect to collect any such sum and get away with it, when the FBI would be turning over every rock west of the Mississippi? He, Romstead, was supposed to pick up the ransom, she'd said. What did that mean? Go into the bank, as the old man had? No, this was supposed to be something entirely different. The only things for sure were that it would be somewhere on the border line between brilliance and insanity, it would involve electronics, and at the end of it, unless he could find some way out of here, he'd be dead, the same as his father.

He wondered if they'd rented this place or if they'd bought it with some of the two hundred and fifty thousand dollars. No doubt after it was over, they'd remove the bars, the steel plate, the mirror, and all the rest of it, and plug up the holes, but if they knew anything about the FBI, they'd better do a good job. With two million paid in ransom and two people dead, the country was going to be sifted, and sifted very fine.

134

There was the sound of a latch being released, and the narrow panel above the chest of drawers slid open. A hand reached in holding a pair of handcuffs and two strips of black cloth. It deposited these on top of the chest. Then the twin barrels of the sawed-off shotgun protruded from the opening, and a voice said, "Romstead, go to the back of the room and face the window."

Dramatic bunch of bastards, Romstead thought, with a real flair for the theater. Next thing he'll gesture with the gun the way they do on TV. He turned and walked back, and stood facing the window. Behind him, the voice went on, "Mrs. Carmody, take these things back there. Blindfold him and handcuff his hands behind him."

"I don't know how to handcuff anybody," she replied. "I must have been absent that day at the Police Academy—"

"Shut up and do as you're told. The cuffs are open. All you have to do is put them around his wrists and push in until the ratchets catch. And if you're fond of him at all, put that blindfold on right."

It wasn't the same voice they'd heard on the intercom; it was a little deeper in pitch and the delivery more aggressive. There was no trace of regional accent that he could hear, so it couldn't be Tex. Then there were at least three. Call this one Top Kick.

He heard her come up behind him and put his hands back. The steel rings closed over his wrists, and then she knotted the blindfold around his head. "Now stand beside him and blindfold yourself," the voice said. Romstead heard her move and then the sound of a bolt being drawn and the turning of a lock.

"Got him heah," another voice said. So that was Tex. That meant he also had a gun of some kind and was covering from the door. Theatrical they might be, but they played

135

it close to the chest when it came to taking chances, though what they thought he could do handcuffed and sightless was beyond him at the moment. The floor was bare except for a throw rug between the beds, and he could hear footsteps coming up behind him. Then another set nearer the door. They were both in the room now.

"You jist go wheah I point you, Sugarfoot," Tex said. His and Paulette's footsteps retreated toward the door, and then something poked into Romstead's back.

"Twelve-gauge double, loaded with number two's," Top Kick said. Romstead made no reply. A big hand grasped his left arm above the elbow and turned him around. "Straight ahead." They crossed the room. He already had the dimensions of that fixed in his mind, and he felt his right arm brush against the door facing just when he expected it. "Right," Top Kick ordered, and pushed his arm. Hallway, Romstead thought, with at least two bedrooms opening onto it. He silently counted the steps. They should be opposite the mirror now, and he pushed the right elbow out just slightly and felt it brush against cloth. So it was curtained on this side.

"Left," Top Kick commanded. So the entrance to the bedroom hallway would be just about opposite the see-through mirror. Romstead turned and began counting again, taking the short steps that would be natural to a sighted person temporarily unable to see but at the same time would be as near exactly two feet as he could make them. He heard a refrigerator motor start up and a dripping sound that could be a leaky faucet. There was the smell of coffee in the air here and the residual odor of fried bacon. The floor was still bare, but he could no longer hear Tex and Paulette ahead of him. Then a screen door opened momentarily, stretching its spring, and Tex said, "Short step down, Honeybunch." The screen snapped back, the latch rattling against the wood.

They'd just gone out, so there must be carpet ahead. Then he was on it, twelve feet from the rear wall of the bedroom hallway.

Three steps in on the carpet, they turned obliquely left, and after nine more Top Kick stopped him and he could feel the threshold under the toe of his shoe. Top Kick pushed the screen door open, still holding the shotgun at his back. "Down," he said.

So the front door of the long room was offset slightly to the left of the hallway door, and they'd had to skirt something, a table or sofa, instead of going straight across. He wondered why he was doing it; it must be purely automatic. The information would be invaluable to the FBI afterward, but who was going to give it to them?

He stepped down carefully and felt a cocoa mat under his foot. Bare planks then for six feet, and then another two steps down onto the grating crunch of pea gravel. There was the resinous fragrance of pine in the air, but no wind at all to give him any aural indication as to how near the surrounding trees were or how dense. No sound of traffic in any direction. A bird he thought was a jay scolded them from somewhere nearby. Sunlight on his head. Remote, peaceful, he thought. Sure, great.

"Left," Top Kick ordered. He turned and began counting again, feeling the rasp of the gravel under his shoes. They were apparently going to another building for some reason, so this direction and distance would be the most important information of all from an investigative standpoint, assuming anybody ever received it. With aerial photography you could cover thousands of square miles in a few hours, looking for two buildings of approximately XY and XY dimensions and separated from each other by Z distance in Z-Prime direction in a clearing in some pines, breaking them down into impossibles, possibles, and probables as fast as you could develop the film.

It seemed highly unlikely that the technological genius didn't know this himself, so the fact that he didn't seem to care was as chilling as the rest of it.

X

THERE were twenty-one steps in the pea gravel, and then he felt a header under his foot. Then five steps across hard-baked ground, and they were on gravel again. Top Kick turned him in a left oblique, and in three steps he felt concrete under his shoes, and simultaneously the sunlight was off his head. Left again, which should put them about ninety degrees from their original direction, and eight steps back. "Hold it," Top Kick ordered. He stopped. Garage, he guessed, oriented in the same direction as the house and approximately fifty-five feet from it. He heard the creaking of springs as an overhead door came down. Right on.

"Interesting trip," Paulette said beside him. "Like a sorority initiation, and about as intelligent."

"Shut up," Top Kick said. "And turn around, both of you."

He did an about-face and heard Paulette turn beside him. Top Kick should be in front of him now, but another gun prodded his back. "Like the monkey said in the lawn mower, don't make no sudden moves, ole buddy." Tex. Somebody was throwing rope around his ankles, hobbling him. He thought of the photograph of his father and was swept with cold rage for an instant but controlled it.

"I'm still here, Romstead," Top Kick said in front of him then. "All right, unlock the cuffs." He felt the handcuffs being lifted. They clicked open. "Put your hands in front of you," Top Kick ordered. He held them out. "You too, Mrs. Carmody." The cuffs closed over his wrists again, and he heard another pair click shut beside him. The pictures, he thought. Realism, artistic detail, the director's touch. Footsteps receded across the concrete. He heard the rustle of cloth somewhere.

"All right, turn them on." This was the intercom voice, presumably Kessler. "And take off the blindfolds."

There was a soft swishing of cloth right beside him. Tex, or whoever it was behind him now, was removing Paulette Carmody's blindfold. He felt fingers working at the knot of his own. Then, from the middle distance somewhere in front, a feminine voice said, "You mean you really would ball that old thing?"

"What an adorable child," Paulette said.

"Who-eee, would I?" It was Tex behind him, all right. "Be like ridin' a Braymer bull." He went on, in imitation of a rodeo announcer, "—comin' out of chute number five on Widow-maker—"

"Get on with it," Top Kick ordered somewhere off to his right. "For Christ's sake, don't you ever think of anything else?"

The blindfold came off then. He blinked, momentarily unable to see anything in the almost painful glare of light burning into his face. Then he could make out that there were four of them, high-intensity floods on standards, two in front and two off to his right. Everything beyond them was indistinct and shadowy, though he could vaguely make out the swing-up door of a two-car garage directly facing him. To his left was a car, a two-door sedan several years old, and on the other side of it, across that whole wall, was a backdrop that appeared to have been made from a cheap plastic dropcloth sprayed with a thin coat of green paint. He looked around in back and saw the wall behind them was covered the same way. He had to admit for the second time that for all their theatricality they didn't miss a bet.

They knew as well as he did that the second set of people to see these pictures was going to be a room full of FBI special agents, and they weren't going to see a hell of a lot. No knotholes, no distinctive grain patterns, stains, old nails, or anything that would identify the place later.

He looked to the right. Tex or Top Kick was standing just far enough back to be well out of the picture, holding the sawed-off shotgun. Six feet two, at least, and heavy in the shoulders, wearing a black jumpsuit and a black hood. By squinting his eyes against the glare he could just make out three more shadowy figures now, slightly behind the lights in front and on his right. One was obviously the girl, not over five five, the second could very easily fit Kessler's description as to build, while the third was as big as the man with the shotgun. They all were dressed the same way.

All those lights weren't necessary for the pictures, of course; they could have used flash bulbs just as well, but the object was to keep him from seeing very much beyond them. His eyes jerked back to the car then; he'd seen something before that hadn't registered at the time. It had two short whip antennas installed on it, one on the roof and one on top of the trunk. And now he saw something else; a half-inch or three-quarters-inch hole had been drilled in the left-hand door, and on the concrete floor beside the car was a steel rod about six feet long threaded at both ends.

"Go ahead, Romstead, take a good look at it," the intercom voice said. "It's yours." The slender figure stepped out of the shadows then, holding a Polaroid camera. He came forward a few steps, sighted through the viewfinder, and moved back a step, presumably to get the handcuffs in the frame.

The camera clicked, and there was a wait while the picture developed. Romstead continued to study the car. The two antennas suggested that basically it was the same operation as before except that it had been transferred to wheels. One would be a transmitter tied to one or more bugging devices inside the car to monitor anything he said or did, while the other would be a receiver for the radio signal that constituted his tether. He'd just grasped the function of the steel rod when Kessler—it was bound to be Kessler—removed the film, peeled off the backing, and studied the result. He nodded. "Perfect the first time." Romstead noted that he was wearing nylon gloves.

"All right, in the car now," Kessler said. "Both of you. Romstead at the wheel." With the shotgun prodding his back, Romstead hobbled over to the car. The other of the two big men opened the door, and he got in behind the wheel, while Paulette was helped into the seat beside him.

"I don't know what we're doing," she said, "unless we're shooting a commercial for mental disease." Nobody paid any attention. Romstead said nothing; he was too intent on what they were doing, probing the setup for any flaw that would offer the slightest ray of hope. Apparently she was to go, too; he hadn't expected that. While the man with the shotgun covered him from Paulette's side, the other unlocked his handcuffs and produced a short length of chain with steel rings at both ends. One cuff was replaced on his left wrist and the other was snapped into one of the rings on the chain. The doors were closed, and Romstead noted there was a hole drilled through the right one too. He'd been right about the rod. The man beside him reached down for it. The end of it appeared in the hole at his left, just over the armrest on the door. It was threaded through the ring at the lower end of the chain, then between Paulette's shackled wrists, and on through the hole in the right-hand door. He heard washers and nuts being applied and the nuts being tightened with wrenches. Nothing, he thought. There was no way they could get out of the car until they were let out.

The rod was half-inch steel, and it passed in front of them between the bottom of the rib cage and the lap, pinning them down and back against the seat. Even without the shackles you couldn't get past it any more than you could get out of the seat with the safety belt fastened. And the doors couldn't be opened, of course, with that rod locking them shut. His right hand was free, and there was enough length to the chain to permit him normal positioning on the wheel with the left, so he could drive, but drive was all he could do. He wouldn't be able to rise from the seat far enough to reach anything else in the car.

"Does she have to go, too?" he asked.

"She shore does." It was Tex who was on the right. "Ain't inny glass in them doors now, Sugarfoot, but you won't be thinkin' about yore hairdo nohow."

She ignored him. One of the light standards was brought around in front of the car to shine in through the windshield. Kessler positioned himself to Romstead's left with the Polaroid. "Left hand up on the wheel, Romstead," he said. "And both of you face this way." They turned. He snapped. Very careful, Romstead thought, not to get any of the exterior of the car. Just the two of us and the backdrop on the other side. When the picture was developed, Kessler nodded with satisfaction. He moved in closer then, shooting downward at an angle to get the detail of the bar and the manacles.

The bar was removed then, and they were taken from the car. Romstead's hands were cuffed behind him again, and they were covered by the ever-vigilant Tex with the shotgun while Kessler photographed something on the floor of the car behind the front seats, using flash bulbs this time because

143

the floods couldn't be brought to bear. When he had two shots to his satisfaction, he nodded to Tex.

"All right, show it to him."

Tex gestured with the gun and nodded. Romstead hobbled forward and looked in around the front seat, which was tilted forward. There was enough peripheral light from the surrounding floods to make it out, though except for one chilling item, none of it made much sense to him. A square aluminum-cased piece of electronics equipment that was obviously homemade because it bore no manufacturer's nameplate was mounted on foam rubber and strapped in place on the floor on the far side. On this side what appeared to be a whole bank of batteries was likewise secured in place, and in between were several interconnecting cables lying loose on the floor. The dynamite was just barely visible, but he was sure that Kessler had framed it in the picture exactly as he wanted it.

There were two bundles of it, one under each seat with only the ends protruding. There were seven sticks in each, strapped together and somehow secured to the floor, and the center stick was armed with a detonating cap whose bare copper wires were connected to some of those running across the floor.

"Just for the pictures," Kessler said behind him. "We'll disarm it until you're on station."

The great-hearted nobility of that, Romstead thought, was somewhat diluted by the fact that one of them would also be in the car to that point, to drive it. He'd be shackled and blindfolded. They had now raised the lid of the trunk, and Kessler was photographing the interior with flash bulbs. The second shot appeared satisfactory.

"All right," he said. "Let him see it."

Tex gestured with the shotgun. Romstead duck-walked around in back. There was more arcane electronics equip-

144

ment foam rubber mounted and lashed in place around the peripheral areas of the trunk, again homemade and inter- connected with lengths of insulated wire and cables, but it was the chest or box that immediately caught his eye and was in its own way as ominous as the dynamite. It took up most of the space in the trunk and was large enough to hold two big suitcases, constructed of welded quarter-inch steel plates lined with asbestos. There was a hinged lid, also of steel plate and asbestos, and a heavy latch on the front of it.

"You see?" Kessler asked.

"Sure," Romstead replied bleakly. "So why should we go?"

"You're misinterpreting it. We just want you to know we're not bluffing; we'll blow it if you force us to. You're a danger- ous man, Romstead; we admit it. You're too much like that old son of a bitch to begin with, and we've learned a little of your background. If you thought we'd hesitate for a min- ute in sending it up because we'd also be blowing the money all over half the state, you'd take the chance. So we took the temptation away from you. If you force us to make it jump, as the French put it, that's too bad, but the money's still safe."

Romstead said nothing, but his face, largely concealed under the blindfold, was intensely thoughtful as they were herded back to the house and into the bedroom. Apparently even a genius could make a small mistake now and then, and maybe if he boasted and embroidered long enough, he might make a bigger one.

He lay stretched out on the bed looking at the passbook and withdrawal slip from the Southland Trust and listening to Kessler's voice on the intercom. At the moment it was addressing Paulette Carmody.

"—just so you won't waste any of our time hoping we don't know what we're talking about and trying to bluff, I'll give

145

it to you fast, chapter and verse. Your husband left an estate of just a little over three million dollars after taxes, all of it to you. About seven hundred thousand of this is real estate, a house in La Jolla, the one in Coleville, some waterfront in Orange County, and the tax-shelter ranch near Elko. About a half million is stock in the land development company he founded in 1953. The rest, pretty close to a million nine hundred thousand, is in bonds, some tax-free—municipals, school district, and so on—some industrials, and some government. The executor of the estate was your husband's younger brother, Jerome Carmody, a La Jolla attorney who's also your attorney.

"The ransom note is addressed to him, to verify the phone call he's already received. It goes out tonight airmail special delivery from some place we'll just say is north of the Tehachapis, along with the pictures to prove we're not lying or bluffing. We want a million eight hundred and thirty thousand from you. It's not his money, so there's no strain. That's what makes this a rather unique kidnapping—you're both paying your own way.

"He'll get the note early tomorrow morning, and he can do the whole thing in one business day. We want delivery of the money day after tomorrow. There are two ways he can do it. He can either mortgage all your holdings for that amount, or he can sell the bonds—"

"Forget it," Paulette Carmody interrupted. She was sitting on the other bed, smoking a filter tip. "The bonds are in my name, and nobody can sell them except me, so he couldn't if he wanted to. And a mortgage form has to be executed before a notary—"

"Nice try," Kessler's voice interrupted in turn. "But we happen to know he has your power of attorney."

Romstead saw her wince a little at this, but she recovered fast. "Which is void the minute I'm dead," she replied. "And

146

as a graduate of Stanford Law School he might conceivably know that."

"But you're not dead, and we've just taken some pictures to prove it. But you will be if we don't get that money, so let's get on with it. He's to deposit it in the Southland Trust and make arrangement for it to be available in cash by day after tomorrow at noon. These things can be expedited when there's an emergency and enough big-money clout behind them.

"And now, Romstead. We want a hundred and seventy thousand. All you have to do, naturally, is sign that withdrawal slip. It's not the bank's money; it's yours, and what you do with it is your business. We've already contacted your friend Carroll Brooks there by telephone—."

"No." It was Romstead's turn to interrupt. "The signature doesn't mean a thing. The bank is obligated to turn the money over only to me or somebody I've designated as my authorized agent."

"Which is exactly what the bank is going to do. Deliver it to you personally." Kessler's voice was smug. "Along with Mrs. Carmody's, since she'll be there too. Carroll Brooks is going to do it."

So now he's made the second one, Romstead thought, but he kept his face impassive, knowing he was being watched through the mirror. "It'll like hell be Brooks," he said scornfully. "You know as well as I do it'll be a special agent of the FBI. You don't think they're going to hold still for this, do you?"

"Oh, I don't doubt the wires to Washington are red-hot right now. But it won't be an FBI agent. That's taken care of."

"Look, use your head, will you? It'll be D. B. Cooper all over again, and if they let you get away with it, every lame-brained creep in the country who can change the batteries in a flashlight is going to become an electronics supercriminal, demanding millions and blowing people up all over the place. This time they're going to get the first one, believe me, if it takes every man in the bureau, and they're going to skin him very slowly with a dull knife and nail his hide on every front page in the country before the imitators can start crawling out of the woodwork."

"If you'll remember," Kessler's voice said, "D. B. Cooper got away with it, precisely because he *was* first and he was qualified."

The bed was beginning to creak on the other side of the wall. Romstead and Paulette Carmody looked at each other and shrugged.

"So sign it, Romstead," the voice went on. "And Mrs. Carmody, just write 'Dear Jerry' comma 'send it' period 'He means business' period on that sheet of paper. I want that note on its way in the next ten minutes."

"And if we don't sign?" Romstead asked, knowing it was a futile question and what the answer would be.

"We bring Mrs. Carmody out here and work on her. We'll do it in front of the intercom, so you can listen."

Romstead thought of the burro. He signed the withdrawal slip and handed her the pen. The sheet of paper was on the nightstand between the beds. The little gasps and outcries filtered through the wall. "I'll be glad to sign it," she said wearily to the intercom, "if you'd just move that riding academy to some other room." She wrote the message he had dictated and put her signature to it. Romstead put the two pieces of paper on top of the chest under the panel, along with the passbook. A hand came through and picked them up. The slide closed and he heard the latch being refastened. The ecstasy on the other side of the wall reached climax, died with one final shriek, and silence returned. Paulette Carmody didn't even try to evade it anymore; maybe, Romstead thought, she had accepted it as part of the process of breaking them down and decided that escape from it was hopeless.

He wondered if the girl could be Debra, but it didn't seem likely. Debra was presumably on heroin, which was supposed to inhibit all sexual desire; if anything had ever eroded this chick's libido, he'd hate like hell to have run into her in a dark alley before she began to cool down. He heard a car start up somewhere in front. The ransom note was on its way.

"What was all this about D. B. Whatsisname?" Paulette asked.

"You remember," Romstead replied. "D. B. Cooper—at least that was supposed to be his name. He started the wave of plane hijackings for money; bailed out over the Pacific Northwest with two hundred thousand dollars, and so far he's either got away with it or he's dead. I'm all for his being dead, and there's a good chance of it. Jumping into heavy timber in the dark will never make you the darling of the insurance companies."

"Oh, sure," she said. "I remember it now. And you figure if this dingy creep gets away with it, electronic extortion will be the latest craze to sweep the country? I see what you mean. And what do you think his chances are of getting away with it?"

"Damned good," Romstead said. "For the short term. They'll get him in the end, of course, but I don't know how much good that'll do us." There was no use raising any false hopes; also, they were being overheard.

There was no further word from the intercom. The day dragged on. At noon two bowls of some kind of stew were handed in through the sliding panel, along with some cans of beer and a carton of Paulette Carmody's brand of cigarettes. They began to hope the girl had gone off with the bearer of the ransom note, but shortly after noon she was back in action again.

"Do you suppose," Paulette asked, "there are any convents that take neophytes my age?"

Romstead smiled but said nothing. He was only half listening to her. He wished Kessler would come on the intercom with his plan for the ransom pickup. There was little or nothing to work on until he did. After a while he went over and spoke into it. "When do we get some idea of what we have to do and where we do it?" There was no reply. Maybe it was going onto a tape. How many were left out there now? There had been complete silence for more than half an hour. Had they all left on business in connection with the pickup? He took off one of the heavy brogues, went over to the chest, and raised the shoe as if to smash in the mirror. The panel slid back, and the barrels of the shotgun came through, aimed at his chest.

"Okay?" a voice asked. It was Top Kick.

"You answered my question," Romstead said. He put the shoe back on and paced the room, goaded by restlessness and frustration.

"I've never been able to understand," Paulette Carmody said, "what the relationship was between you and your father. If there was any."

"There wasn't much," Romstead replied.

"I know. Let's face it, parenthood must have weighed about as heavily on him as it does on the average ram or stallion or seed bull, and somehow I can't quite see him as today's suffering blob of guilt on the head candler's couch weeping and beating his chest and asking, 'What did I do wrong?' He supported you until you were old enough to support yourself, and if he happened to run into you now and then he'd buy you a drink, but that was about it. But still he liked you and admired your athletic ability, and it all seemed to turn out all right. Did you resent the fact you hardly ever saw him? Did you feel rejected?"

"No." He stopped pacing and thought about it. People had asked him the same question before, and he'd never known how to answer it. There had been respect between them and a good deal of mutual admiration, but they'd simply never needed each other. Maybe, actually, neither of them had ever really needed anybody; the self-sufficiency was inherited, built in, and perhaps that was the only thing they shared.

"Have you got a girl?" she asked.

"Yes. Quite a girl."

"I'd like to meet her sometime. But God help her if she ever marries you. You're simply too much like him."

He shrugged. "That's what Kessler said."

"And I wonder what he meant. They killed your father in the end, but I'm not sure that's all that happened. They're very, very careful."

He started to tell her that you always had to be careful of people who didn't have much more to lose, but there seemed no point to it. She was tough-minded and realistic enough to handle it, but why belabor the matter?

They were given some more of the stew for dinner. The overhead light was turned on at dusk. Sleeping under it was difficult, but, Romstead reflected, it would have been a little difficult anyway. All they could do was endure it and wait. It was eleven o'clock the next morning when they heard a car drive up in front. A few minutes later Kessler came on the intercom.

"You'll be glad to hear that Jerome Carmody and the bank have agreed to the two million," he said, "and to the terms of delivery."

"What about the police?" Romstead asked. "And the FBI?"

"They swear they haven't called them in, and there's nothing in any of the papers or on TV; but of course they have. I have no doubt that right now whole roomfuls of them are playing the telephone tapes over and over and tearing their hair out in handfuls trying to get voice patterns or something in the background. A cordless vibrator against the throat doesn't help them much."

Keep going, Romstead thought; embroider. Egomania's about all we've got going for us—egomania and greed.

"At first we thought of having Jerome Carmody deliver the money," Kessler's voice went on, "but we found out he's got a serious heart condition, and I don't want somebody crapping out on a freeway at seventy miles an hour with two million dollars of my money in his car—"

"You ought to guard against that streak of sentimentality," Paulette interrupted.

"Shut up, if you want to hear this. So we decided on Brooks. He works for the bank, so the bank is simply delivering your own money to you. Two of us have seen him up close, so they can't run in an FBI ringer on us.

"They have the pictures and the facts of life as they are. You'll be on the leash, with enough explosive in the car to blow it all to hell and only the transmitted radio signal keeping the detonating circuit from closing and setting it off. I'm using a lower frequency this time for longer range of operation and so there'll be no reception blind spots when you're behind hills or in canyons. And I won't be at the transmitter; that'll be in another part of the forest and remote-controlled itself. They can locate it with direction finders and get up there where it is with mules in five or six hours, but why would they? If they turn it off, *they'll* kill you. They've been warned that any deviation at all from the procedure I've given them and you'll go up, and they know that anywhere along the line we can get a look at the vehicle to be sure it's Brooks in it.

"Delivery of the money will be in the Mojave Desert between Barstow and Las Vegas. If any other vehicle follows him off the highway or if there's a plane or helicopter in sight anywhere the deal is off and we go back to square one and start over—"

"All right," Romstead interrupted. "Let's say they give you that—Brooks alone, nobody following him. You've got enough clout at this point that they probably have to. But for Christ's sake, use your head. In the first place, you should know as well as I do that Brooks is going to be in constant contact with the FBI by radio. The United States government has access to maybe a little electronics expertise itself. Second, the car, whatever it is, is going to be carrying a homing device of some kind so they can track it with direction finders, and in the third place—and this is the one you can't beat—wherever you take delivery you're going to be quarantined. You're going to be surrounded on all sides to the point of saturation by police, sheriff's deputies from a half dozen counties, and FBI agents. They'll block every exit a jackrabbit could squeeze through. And don't think they can't."

"Of course they can." Kessler sounded amused. "Blockade, cordon, or whatever you want to call it, is one of the oldest law enforcement tactics in the world, and it works—provided you know what area to blockade. They won't, until it's too late, and it's a long way from Barstow to Las Vegas. Over a hundred and fifty miles to be exact. . . . All right, pass him the maps."

This latter was obviously addressed to whoever was on the other side of the mirror. Romstead went over by the chest. The panel slid open. Oil company highway maps of California and Nevada were deposited on top of the chest, followed by a large sheet of white paper folded several times and some thumb tacks. The panel closed, and Romstead heard the latch being fastened.

"Unfold the large map, and thumbtack it to the wall," Kessler ordered, "so you can follow this."

Romstead unfolded it. It was meticulously hand-drawn and inked, and he assumed it was a large-scale blowup of some section of the highway from Barstow to Las Vegas. He stuck it to the wall between the beds with the tacks.

"Those highway maps you've got don't show all the desert roads," Kessler said. "Mine does, even the ungraded ones. It's drawn to scale, and I've run all those roads myself, the ones we're going to use. It extends for thirty miles east and west along a section of Highway Fifteen east of Barstow and covers the area from ten miles south to twenty miles north of the highway, or nine hundred square miles in all.

"Now. Brooks doesn't know yet where he's supposed to go, only that he's to use an open Toyota Land Cruiser so we can see there's no FBI joker concealed in it. Ten minutes before he's due to leave the bank with the money he'll get a phone call, the last one, which will throw all the Efrem Zimbalist Juniors into a third-degree flap trying to trace it. It will be long-distance-dialed from one of a room-long bank of pay phones at Los Angeles International by a girl in a wig and dark glasses, and the message will take five seconds, so lots of luck—"

"Accomplished young lady," Paulette Carmody murmured. "She operates vertically, too."

Kessler paid no attention. He went on. "It'll simply tell him to go to Barstow, which will take less than four hours, and register at the Kehoe Motel under the name of George Mellon. There's a package there for him that was delivered two days ago by a parcel service with instructions to hold for arrival. It's a radio receiver, single channel, crystal-controlled. The object of all this scrimshaw, of course, is to keep the Zimbalists from getting hold of it enough in advance of when he has to use it so they can find out what frequency it's tuned to. They'll descend on the Kehoe the minute they hear this, of course, and they'll have the receiver before Brooks gets there; but there's still not time, and they wouldn't have the lab facilities in Barstow anyway. There's a note with it telling Brooks to proceed east on Highway Fifteen with the phones plugged into the receiver for further instructions."

Romstead broke in. "It won't do any good. They'll be in front of him and behind him, and even if they can't pick up the channel themselves, they'll see where he leaves the highway."

"Sure." Kessler went on. "But it takes time to surround an area of several hundred square miles. And when they do, they're going to surround the wrong area. Brooks is going to leave the highway headed south, but you're going to be waiting for him on the opposite side, to the north. In that six hundred square miles."

Romstead whistled soundlessly. That was going to be rough to handle if he could pull it off. But how could he?

"The radio message," Kessler went on, "will simply tell him to take that exit I've got marked A on the map and proceed five point eight miles straight down that road, where he will receive further instructions. But not by radio this time. One of us will have him under visual surveillance with a telescope—we'll have two of them in operation, with our own communications setup. If anybody follows him off the highway, the whole deal is off. And after a little over four miles he's in very rough country and completely out of sight of the highway.

"When the five point eight turns up on his odometer, there will be a pickup truck parked a little distance off the road, just a dusty, beat-up old truck like a thousand others in the area. It's stolen, and so are the plates. The ignition key will be in it, along with a note and a change of clothes, Levi's, blue shirt, and rancher's straw sombrero. He's to leave his Toyota there, change clothes, transfer the two suitcases of money to the truck, and go on in it. After a mile he takes a road to the right; four and a half miles farther on there'll be another road running right again, back toward the highway. He'll cross the highway at that exit I've got marked B and continue on to where he'll meet you in a little over six miles. Even if the highway is still running bank to bank with FBI men, they'll never recognize him."

"Except," Romstead said, "that they'll have a complete description of the new vehicle, including the license number, plus the information that he's now headed north, and on which road. When he transfers the money to the truck, he'll also transfer the FBI's communication gear and the squealer —the radio beacon. . . ." His voice trailed off then, and he felt a little chill begin between his shoulder blades.

"Sure he will," Kessler agreed. "Only now they're completely useless. I've been monitoring that whole end of the spectrum with some very sophisticated gear, and before he's even left the highway the first time, I'll know his communications and beacon frequencies. And from the time he starts south, before the transfer, I'll be sitting right on both of them with a couple of wide-band jamming signals. Communications blackout."

XI

HE'D long since lost all track of time, but Romstead guessed they'd been off pavement for more than an hour now. They must be approaching the pickup area from the back. The road was rough, with a great many turns, and they were driving fast, bouncing and swaying while dust filtered into the vehicle, whatever it was, and rocks and gravel clattered against the undercarriage. The heat was stifling, very near to unbearable. He was blindfolded and gagged, his hands cuffed behind him, and his ankles were bound with rope. Paulette Carmody was beside him. They were lying on a mattress in what he believed was the bed of a pickup truck with a steel or aluminum cover. He had raised his feet when he was first shoved in, hours ago, and had felt the cover above them, too low to be the roof of a panel truck. A panel would be conspicuous out here, anyway, where everybody had a pickup.

They hadn't used the sedative drugs this time, he supposed, because there could be no certainty he'd regain consciousness in time. They were efficient, all right; he had to admit that in spite of the rage and the desire to get his hands on Kessler and kill him. Sometime later today it would be seventy-two hours since they'd been kidnapped, and not once had he seen one of the four of them as anything but a shadowy figure in a black hood; he couldn't describe any of their vehicles, the exterior of either of the buildings, or even the interior except for one room that would be completely done over after the thing was pulled off.

He wondered at these precautions, since it was certain they'd be killed anyway for knowing Kessler's identity. More embroidery? A flair for drama? Or did they think he was stupid enough to be lulled by all this window dressing into an idiot's belief that they would be turned loose afterward? No, he decided, it was more likely the others had insisted on it in case he should escape, as impossible as that might be. He didn't know any of them, though he had a hunch that Top Kick might be the Delevan that Murdock had mentioned, the corrupt private detective who'd done a stretch in San Quentin for extortion.

They were slowing. The vehicle came almost to a stop, turned, and began to crawl, swaying and lurching over uneven ground as though they had left the road. This continued for a minute or two, and then they stopped. The noise of the motor ceased. He heard a door slam on another car nearby. They must be there. One of them had driven the deadly two-door sedan, and this was their rendezvous point. He heard the driver of their vehicle get out and then the sound of voices, though he could make out nothing that was said. Then the tailgate of the pickup was dropped, and he heard the door being opened.

"We're here." It was Top Kick's voice. "All out."

He heard Paulette being helped out; then they were hauling on his legs. He managed to get his feet on the ground and stand, swaying awkwardly and stretching cramped muscles after the hours of constriction. He could feel the sun beating on his head now as it had on the metal cover over them.

"Pit stop," Top Kick said. "You're going to be in that car quite awhile. This way, Mrs. Carmody; nobody'll watch."

"You're shore you don't need no help?" Tex asked. He'd

be my second choice, Romstead thought, after Kessler. Just five minutes alone in a locked room.

"Get on with those antennas," Top Kick ordered. "We haven't got all day." So they'd removed them for the trip. Smart. Anybody might notice a car with two whip antennas.

Two pairs of footsteps went away and one came back. The bonds about his ankles were loosened so he could hobble. "Cover him while I unlock the cuffs," Top Kick said. The handcuffs were removed and then replaced with his hands in front.

"Okay, Mrs. Carmody?" Top Kick called.

"Yes," she replied from somewhere off to his left. They had removed her gag. Her voice was strained, and he could sense the shakiness under it. She was fighting hard to keep from breaking. "Keep him covered," Top Kick said, and went to get her. They came back. Top Kick took him by the arm and guided him off to one side. The ground was rocky and uneven. "Fire at will, Romstead. She's still blindfolded anyway."

He urinated. Top Kick led him back, shuffling in his hobbles. He heard the rattle of tools against metal over to his right. Then in a minute Tex said, "Okay, the ears is on. You can do yore's, an' welcome to the mother-lovers."

"Right. Watch him."

He heard the door of the car being opened. In back of him, Tex said, "'Member how he said, y'heah? Watch that relay when you turn the radio on. Be sure it pulls over an' holds tight as a bull's ass in flytime before you start wirin' them caps."

"I know how to do it," Top Kick's voice said from inside the car.

"I shore as hell hope you do, ole buddy, 'cause we'd all go with you. Be hamburger for miles around."

Romstead realized then that Paulette was right beside

him. A hand groped along his arm and slid down it to his. Hers was trembling. He squeezed it. You did what you could. It wasn't much.

"All right, the baby's born," Top Kick said. "Put her in."

She was whispering, very softly, against his ear. "I won't—I won't break down—in front of—these goddamned animals. . . ." Then she was being led away. In a moment that car door slammed.

The shotgun prodded his back, and somebody had hold of his arm. He was led forward and stopped, and he could feel the car against his right arm. Somebody was untying his ankles. "In you go," Top Kick said. He slid in on the seat. The door closed. The handcuffs were unlocked then, and one was resnapped about his left wrist. He heard the rattle of chain, and then the sound of the rod's being fed through the hole in the left door. It pushed past his stomach and went on. There was the rattle of nuts and washers and then a little pop when the thin sheet metal of the door buckled slightly under the pressure of the tightening nuts as wrenches were applied. "That's good," Top Kick said.

Fingers worked at the knot at the back of his neck, and the gag was removed. His jaws ached, and his mouth was dry as he worked the tight ball of cloth out of his mouth.

"Leave the blindfolds on until I tell you," Top Kick said beside him. Then, apparently to Tex, "All right, take it away."

Romstead heard the other vehicle start up and move off, going toward their rear. In a minute it apparently stopped, for he could hear the idling motor some distance away but no longer fading.

"All right, remember what he told you," Top Kick said. "You're out of sight of the road here, so you won't be able to see it either. It's off to your right, just the other side of this hill. Brooks won't know where you are, but he'll be watching his odometer and when the specified mileage turns up, he honks his horn, twice, as he goes by here, if there's nobody else in sight, ahead or behind. When you hear him, start up, go on around the end of the hill, and you'll be on the road with him ahead of you. He'll see you in the mirror, and after a mile he'll pull off the road twenty or thirty feet to the right and stop. You go on by, and he'll fall in and follow you a quarter mile behind. Check your odometer here. At five point three miles from this point you stop. Brooks has instructions to stop a hundred yards behind you. You'll both be in the field of a telescope, and a hand will be on the switch of that transmitter that's keeping you from blowing up, so remember it.

"He walks forward with the two suitcases, puts them in that steel box in the trunk, and latches it. If he takes one more step, up the side of the car toward you, the whole thing goes up. If he tries to pass you a gun or a tool of some kind, she blows. He's been told all that already. So he goes back to his pickup, turns around, and heads back to the highway. It'll be hours before he gets there; that's been explained to you—the rock slide. He'll have to walk most of the way.

"The rest of it's marked on your map, the turns you make and the distances. We'll pick you up and disarm the thing before you go out of transmitter range. It'll be dark very shortly after then, and we'll be out of the country in a different set of vehicles before they even find out what direction we went. Okay?"

"If you could call it that," Romstead said.

"So you can take off the blindfolds when I sing out. Then just wait." Footsteps receded. Sing out, Romstead thought. Ex-seaman. So far, that was the only slip Top Kick had made.

"Okay," Top Kick called, some distance behind them. At the same moment a car door slammed, and he heard the other vehicle accelerate in low gear, going away. He yanked off the blindfold, winced at the sudden glare, and craned to look back. The vehicle was already out of sight around the curve of the hill, but he could still hear it. It had apparently turned when it came out on the road, for it seemed to be fading away in the same direction they were headed.

He looked around then. Paulette Carmody had put her head down and pulled off her blindfold with her manacled hands; but her eyes were still closed, and he could see tears on the curve of her cheek. Her hair was in disarray from removing the cloth. He reached over with his free right hand and did his awkward best to smooth it back in place. He squeezed her shoulder then and could feel her trembling.

"Thank you, Eric." Her head was still lowered. She sobbed once and went on shakily, "I—I'm so ashamed—"

"Of what? You didn't break."

"B-but I almost did. You'll never know how close it was. I ha-have to tell you. I wanted to throw myself on the ground and grab them by the legs and b-beg them to send you alone. Kill you—save me. Oh, Christ—"

"Well, you didn't, kid, and that's where they start from when they give out the medals. Wanting to but not doing it." He felt like a sadist for not telling her there was a faint ray of hope even yet because it was Carroll Brooks who was bringing the money, but it was too soon to begin the charade. He glanced at his watch. It was three fifteen. Far too soon. That great extemporizer with the chain-lightning mind wouldn't even have reached Barstow yet, and it would wreck everything if he said a word before they were irretrievably committed to the delivery. They'd call it off, and they'd have to go through the whole thing again somewhere else with another man bringing the money. And they wouldn't be beyond the point of no return until after Carroll had made the change of vehicles and recrossed the highway, headed north.

He didn't have the faintest idea when that would be because he didn't know how far east of Barstow they were. They could be in Nevada for all he knew. He'd have to wait until Carroll went by here to be sure. It would only take a few words, anyway, to plant the doubt.

Maybe he could whisper it right against her ear. No. Let it ride. He didn't know how many bugging devices there were in the car, what kind they were, or how sensitive. And it was only the slimmest of hopes anyway. Maybe it would be even crueler to mention it.

Her hands were tightly clasped together. She took a deep, shaky breath and said, "It was different back in the room. It was unreal—it wasn't actually going to happen—and now it has." She shook her still-lowered head. "I'm almost afraid to breathe."

"No. Forget that," he said—with more confidence than he felt. "It's set up for electrical detonation and won't go off unless he does it." He saw they'd brought her purse. It was on the seat between them. He fumbled it open with his right hand and brought out the cigarettes. Shaking one out, he located her lighter, fired it up, and held it between her lips. She puffed and inhaled deeply. If she had anything to do, he thought, it would help.

"You're in charge of reading the odometer," he said. "Check it now and add five point three so you can watch it and tell me when it's coming up."

"Right." She took another puff of the cigarette, and when he removed it, she lowered her face and tried to wipe the tears from her cheek by dabbing it against her sleeve. He transferred the cigarette to his other hand and found a tissue in her purse. When he blotted at them, she smiled wanly. "You know, I think you are a gentle man. Maybe I won't tell your girl to get the hell out before it's too late."

163

He made no reply. He was studying the desolate and sun-blasted country around them, trying to guess where Kessler would be. Judging from the time and the shadows of the few cacti around them, they must be facing approximately north. They seemed to be on the floor of an immense valley, perfectly flat except for an occasional small hill or rocky ridge and, a few miles farther west, three higher hills shaped like truncated cones. He could be on one of those, he thought; he'd want to be as high as possible, but still not on anything isolated and conspicuous. He turned to look back. It was rougher there, in the distance, at least, a naked badland of much higher ridges and towering buttes, but that might be on the other side of the highway. Ahead of them, at a distance he guessed must be ten miles or so, the country began to rise again and break up into a lunar landscape of desolate ridges and canyons.

He could see nothing to the right because of the hill be-hind which they were concealed. He leaned down to look up through the window and saw it wasn't much more than a stony hummock some twenty feet high and perhaps a hundred yards long dotted with big boulders and here and there a cactus struggling for survival in the flinty ground.

He wondered if the other side might be where the charge was placed to drop a rock slide in front of Carroll's car so he'd have to walk back to the highway, as Kessler had said. The terrain here, however, was so flat he could drive around it, so it must be farther back. His thoughts broke off then. A car was coming. It couldn't be this soon, could it? No, it was approaching from the north. Well, even in this God-forsaken place there must be a little traffic on the roads. It went on by, traveling fast.

They waited. It was 4 P.M. . . . 4:30. The sun beat down. Heat waves shimmered above the desert floor, distorting everything in the distance. He looked around and saw Paulette had her eyes closed, her lower lip clenched between her teeth, silently crying. He put a hand on her arm and squeezed. She nodded *thank you* but didn't trust herself to try to speak.

It was five. A quarter of six.

They heard him coming.

It had to be. The car was coming up from the south. As it approached at moderate speed, he was conscious that he was holding his breath. It was going past now on the other side of the hummock. Still going. Maybe they'd called it off— Then it came, two short blasts of the horn. He exhaled softly as he hit the ignition switch and started up, automatically checking the odometer again as he'd already done a half dozen times before. It would read 87.7 at the stopping point.

The ground ahead was uneven and rock-strewn, and he eased forward at a crawl, feeling the tightness in his throat at every lurch and sway. It wasn't the dynamite as such or even the detonating caps he was thinking of. They'd be cushioned. It was that relay. How strong was the current that was keeping it pulled over against the tension of its spring? Well, it would be cushioned, too, he thought.

They came around the end of the hummock and onto the road. It wasn't even graded, just a track running north across the level floor of the desert. The old pickup truck was ahead, a little less than a quarter mile and going very slowly, waiting for him. As he closed the distance, it began to pick up a little. Now? he thought. No, wait'll you pass and be absolutely sure it's Carroll. And it'd be a lot more effective if he could get Paulette to give him a cue to lead into it. Coming on cold with it could have a very phony ring, and Kessler, whatever else he was, was no fool.

The pickup was pulling off now. It stopped a scant twenty feet from the road. Romstead slowed. The driver was hatless, and he'd taken off his sunglasses as he leaned out the window to wave, a man with prematurely gray hair and a lean, alert face stamped with a questing intelligence. During their college years Brooks had wanted to be an actor; his only drawback was an inability, or unwillingness, to learn lines, when it was so much more fun to make them up himself. Give him one cue, and he'd ad-lib the whole play. Romstead sighed.

He slowed a little as the pickup fell in behind them. They had only four miles now to the transfer point. The road ran straight ahead across absolutely flat terrain unbroken by any irregularity except for another low hummock or stony ridge far ahead. Kessler had chosen his spot well. With his telescope he could see for miles in any direction across a landscape where nothing could be concealed. They and the pickup were the only vehicles anywhere in the immensity of it. Three miles.

Okay, he thought; air time. He began to whistle "Sweet Georgia Brown," drumming the beat on the wheel. Paulette Carmody raised her head and stared at him in horrified disbelief. He grinned and winked and cupped an ear in the listening gesture.

"My God, aren't you even scared?" she asked.

"Relax," he replied. He had no idea where the bug was, but it didn't matter. He'd be heard. And of course, there'd be another in the trunk to monitor Brooks. "They're not going to blow it while the money's still in the pickup, that's for sure. And I don't think they're going to blow it afterward either."

She swallowed, and moistened her lips. He could see her wanting desperately to hope but not daring to. "What—what do you mean?"

166

"Intelligence slipup. Theirs is pretty good, but they didn't go quite far enough. They investigated you, and Jerome Carmody, and me and my background, but they should have done just a little checking into Brookie's background, too."

Two point six to go. Her eyes were imploring. Her lips formed "Please," but nothing came out. He went on. "That's the reason I kept nudging him on with that bat sweat about its being impossible, that the FBI would find a way to ring in one of their men. I wanted him to insist on Brooks and get him. You see, Brookie and I used to be a team in an outfit that forgot more dirty tricks last week than Kessler'll know in a lifetime—"

She nodded, and said in a small voice. "I thought so. The CIA."

"You said it; I didn't. Anyway, we operated in Central and South America because we're both bilingual in Spanish and English. We've been through kidnappings before—from both sides of the fence, whether you agree with it or not. So I don't think they're going to blow this car. I know what I'd do if they had Brookie, and our minds always seemed to operate along the same lines. I would have told you before, but it had to wait till they were committed. They can't call it off now, so they're stuck with Brookie. Right, Kessler?"

It was less than two miles now. She had lowered her head again, and her hands were clenching and unclenching. He looked back. Carroll was hanging a steady quarter mile behind. The road, if you could call it that, ran straight on with nothing to break the monotony of the desert floor except the low stony ridge coming up on their right. The seeds of doubt should be planted now, they had a few minutes to germinate, and now it would all depend on Carroll. He reached out a hand and squeezed Paulette's arm. She raised her head, tried to force a semblance of a smile, and checked the odometer again. He glanced at it. It read 86.8. Nine-tenths to go.

He looked off to the left toward the three hills that resembled truncated cones. One of those was bound to be where Kessler was. There was no real elevation anywhere off to the right, and anyway that hummock or ridge was coming up on that side not more than two hundred yards off the road—

Panic hit him then for an instant, along with a surge of guilt and rage at his own stupidity. Maybe it was already too late, and he'd killed the friend behind him. He'd been so intent on the other thing he'd missed it entirely. He'd blown it. The odometer read 87.1, and the .1 was already past the center and moving up. He cut the throttle and rode the brake. It would look like a crash stop to them, so he said, "Damn! Almost overran it."

Paulette Carmody jerked her head around and was opening her mouth to speak when he got a finger to his lips and gave a violent shake of the head. He looked at the odometer again as they came to a full stop, and then at the nearest point on the ridge. Call it nine hundred yards. Maybe he'd saved it. Just maybe. The rifle would be sighted in for two hundred, and changing the elevation on the scope was guesswork without a few rounds to check it, but the man, whichever one he was, was plenty good. He'd seen some of his work.

How in hell could he have fallen for that rockslide story? He'd heard the car go off toward the north, hadn't he, and then a little later another car go by them headed south? Kessler couldn't keep that communications frequency jammed for very long at a time or the FBI would use their direction finders to zero in on his jamming transmitter, and anyway they had to keep Carroll from getting back to the highway for longer than an hour or two. He should have seen all that, but he'd been too wrapped up in some way to save his own neck.

He looked back through the settling dust of their passage.

168

The pickup was stopped a hundred yards behind them, and Carroll Brooks was getting out.

Pal, he thought, this could be the biggest role you ever played; just pick up your cues and ad-lib the hell out of it.

XII

PAULETTE was still looking at him imploringly. He pointed toward the ridge and crooked his index finger in a triggering motion. She shuddered and closed her eyes, and he realized she was very close to the edge. This kind of tension continued long enough could break anybody. He looked back again. Carroll had the two big suitcases out now; he picked them up and started toward them. They seemed to be heavy; well, no doubt they were. Two million dollars, in any denominations, would be a lot of tightly packed paper. Shadows were lengthening; it would be dark in less than an hour.

He was getting closer. Fifty yards now. Romstead stuck his head out the window and called, "*¿Qué tal, amigo? Hace muchos años.*" Carroll didn't know a word of Spanish, but his reply, if any, wouldn't be distinguishable at that distance. The other appeared to shake his head, but he said nothing. He came on.

He was at the back of the car now. He put the suitcases down. "Been a long time, Brookie," Romstead said out the window. He never called him Brookie. "That crummy *barrio* back of Lake Titicaca, wasn't it?" Carroll was the only one he'd ever told about it.

"When they sent Ramirez back to us in two boxes and a rolled poncho?" Brooks asked. "Who could ever forget it?" He was ready. He raised the lid of the trunk. No doubt he'd seen the pictures and knew what the steel box was for, but

170

another look at it would help. And he'd be speaking right into the bug.

"What did you use?" Romstead asked. "Thermite or acid?"

"Acid," Brooks replied with no hesitation at all. "Fooling around with ignition hardware for thermite gets too complicated."

"Nitric?" Romstead, winking at him in the mirror.

"Sulphuric." Brooks set the first suitcase in very carefully, as though it contained eggs. "Two liters in each bag, side by side in scored flasks. If he blows it, he's going to have two million dollars' worth of beautiful green slime."

"With bubbles," Romstead said. "Hold the second bag a minute. There's a sniper on that ridge. I goofed and didn't get it in time. His rifle will be sighted in for two hundred yards, and I make it between eight and nine, but he's an artist. He won't open up till you've got the trunk closed, so slam it fast, hit the dirt on this side of the car, and I'll back up and give you cover to the truck."

"No." Brooks shook his head. "He'd blow it sure as hell then. To get me. If I make it back to the highway, he's had it."

"I don't think he will," Romstead said.

Brooks was lifting in the other case. He closed the lid of the steel box as though he had all the time in the world. "Don't bet on it," he said. He slammed the trunk shut then, whirled, and started to run, bent low and zigzagging.

He apparently caught the rifleman as much by surprise as he did Romstead, for he'd covered nearly twenty yards before the first shot came. A puff of dust erupted just ahead of him but a good ten feet short of the road, followed by the crack of the gun up on the ridge. By this time Romstead had jammed the car into reverse and was trying to overhaul him. There was a second explosion of dirt in the road itself but still five feet short as Brooks veered wildly to the right.

Romstead was closing now, but he saw he was going to do more harm than anything. The way Brooks was hurtling back and forth across the road in his evasive tactics he'd be more likely to run over him than help him. He had less than thirty yards to go now anyway.

There was the sound of another shot, but Romstead couldn't see where it had hit; it must have gone high. Then Brooks went down, still twelve or fifteen feet short of the truck. The sound of the shot followed. Romstead cursed and slammed the car into reverse again, but Brooks was up almost instantly. He was hobbling and holding his left leg. He lunged for the door of the pickup, and as he yanked it open, the glass in it shattered. He made it behind the wheel. The pickup sprang forward in a wide turn, bouncing over the uneven ground off the road, and then was accelerating as it drew away.

There was no telling how badly he was hurt or whether he might pass out from loss of blood before he could make it to the highway. Romstead's face was savage as he slammed the car into gear. It leaped forward. He gunned it and heard rubber shriek. He didn't know whether the rifleman would try to get him or not. If it were Top Kick he might; he'd know how to disarm the explosive charge. He could take it over here, though it was dangerously close to where the country would be swarming with police ten miles to the south. And Tex was stupid enough, on the other hand, for anything to be possible. They were doing sixty-five when they came abreast of the near end of the ridge. He became conscious then that Paulette was shouting something at him, over and over.

"Aren't you going back? For the love of God, aren't you going back?"

"No," he said. Then the wing window shattered just in front of her. A hole appeared in it, it cracked in a crazy pattern like a spider web, and fragments of glass showered into the car. She screamed, took a long, shuddering breath, and screamed again. She slumped forward. Romstead heard another bullet strike the car somewhere else as they tore ahead. They couldn't go back. The minute he started to turn around, Kessler would blow it. He'd have nothing to lose then, acid or no acid, because the money would be gone anyway, and he'd have everything to gain. They knew who he was, and even if he got out of here, the FBI would pick him up within days. But as long as he was going ahead, into their country, they'd hesitate to blow it.

At least for a few more minutes, he thought. Then they'd begin to have second thoughts about it, whether anybody would destroy two million dollars as casually as that; once this credibility gap appeared, it would widen, and he had to break his way out of the car before it did because they'd be able to hear what he was up to. Of course, there was an excellent chance that what he was going to do would blow it up anyway, but after a certain point you'd reached saturation in the possibilities for disaster, so one more didn't matter much.

He looked back. He couldn't see the pickup anymore, but there was too much dust to be sure it hadn't stopped or gone off the road. There appeared to be no other dust plume behind them yet, but again you couldn't be certain of that either through the shifting curtains of their own. Rougher country was just ahead; somewhere in there he should find what he was looking for.

But he was going too fast. They hit a bump, and for an instant all four wheels were off the ground; he seemed to be somewhere far off, watching with clinical detachment and arriving at a decision: if they came down without exploding, he'd better cool it a little. He eased the throttle. There was a rocky ridge on the right now with a scattering of large boulders on its slopes, and just ahead the road dived into a shallow canyon between two of them. He cut his speed to thirty, and then to twenty, as he entered it. Kessler couldn't see them now, no matter where he was. But he could still hear, he thought.

Up ahead the slopes on each side closed in and steepened, but he saw what he was looking for before that. He slammed on the brakes. Along the base of the slope to his left, just off the road, were several large boulders, some bigger than the car, shrugged off the hillside in some seismic upheaval of the geologic past. They were in a variety of shapes, but one of them had a configuration he thought would do. He put the car into reverse, shot backward a few yards, and pulled over beside it. This side was practically vertical, with a slight outcropping approximately where he wanted it. He leaned his head out the window and looked down.

They'd left at least an inch and a half of the threaded rod protruding beyond the washer, and the nut on this side. He'd have to attack it in reverse, however; going ahead would push the rod back against them if he managed to tear it at all, and it could cut them in two. He pulled ahead about ten feet, cut the wheels, and looked back to line it up. Paulette Carmody had raised her head now and was staring at him in a sort of benumbed wonder, unable even to guess what he might do next. He shifted into reverse and came back, hard, turning the wheel a little more to wipe the door right across the jagged and nearly vertical face of the rock.

There was a screech of rending metal as the door handle came off, tearing away a section of the skin. But his wheels were spinning now, digging in with a whining sound of their own. His angle was too steep, and he was jammed against it. He shifted and shot ahead four or five feet and started back again.

"Good God in heaven," Paulette Carmody said, and shut her eyes. He tried not to think of that relay himself. They came into it with a crash and another shriek of metal, and he gunned it hard to keep going. The door buckled in toward them; they hung for a second or two, and in this fleeting hiatus in the sounds of destruction marred only by the high whining of the wheels he heard Paulette praying beside him, "—hallowed be Thy name, Thy kingdom come—" Then they were moving again, to another keening of agonized metal, and when they lost contact with the face of the boulder the rod was some four inches in front of him, and he could see the long tear in the material lining the inside of the door. He stopped and looked out the window.

The rod had ripped through the sheet metal for at least five inches in a widening tear that was now nearly the width of the washer, and one side of the washer was already in it. He caught the rod with both hands, palms up in a weight lifter's hold, braced his elbows against the back of the seat, and heaved. At first nothing happened. He relaxed, came up again, and then put his whole strength into one burst of upward pressure. There was a sound like a breaking guitar string as the washer popped through and the rod bent upward. He tore it through the composition material lining the door, slipped his ring off it, and pushed the end of it from between Paulette's shackled wrists. It wouldn't go on out through the hole in the right-hand door, of course, because the nut and washer were still on it and jammed now beyond removal by anything short of a hacksaw, but it didn't matter.

Paulette Carmody's eyes were open now, and she was looking at him in a sort of numb blending of awe and gratitude and returning hope. She started to speak; he cut her off with an abrupt, almost savage gesture for silence, shoved the door open on her side, and waved—*get the hell out, run.* She looked startled, almost as if she were as much afraid of him

175

now as of the dynamite, scrambled out of the seat, and began to run along the edge of the road.

He shoved at his door. It was jammed. He was about to slide over and get out on her side when it suddenly gave way and fell open as much as swung open. The screws in the upper hinge had been sheared off by the pressure. He shoved it out of the way, got out, and pulled the seat forward.

Kessler had long since figured out what he was up to, and if he were going to blow it at all, he'd do it within the next few minutes. By this time he must have serious doubts regarding that moonshine about the acid, and anyway he'd send it up to prevent their escape. No amount of money was going to save him if they got away to identify him. The sun was gone out of the canyon entirely now, and the light was poor on the floor behind the seats; he could just make out the detonating caps and their wires. They weren't soldered, thank God; merely twisted. He pulled the first one loose, and then the other. It was disarmed.

He sighed, and his knees felt weak for a moment in testimony to the amount of tension they'd been under for hours now, and then it was gone, and he was plowing ahead. He pulled the two detonating caps free, straightened, and threw them back up the road, indifferent as to whether they exploded or not. They didn't. He yanked at the webbing holding down the two bundles of dynamite, tore it loose, and set the explosive out on the ground at the base of the boulder. Paulette Carmody had climbed a short distance up the slope a hundred yards away and was watching him from behind another big rock. He gestured that she could come back now.

He tore off the straps holding the piece of electronics equipment in place and hauled it out. All the interconnecting wires, several still fast to dangling clusters of batteries like the fruit of some electronic grapevine, seemed to converge into one cable at the back of it. He caught it by the cable and swung it against the boulder, batteries and all. Parts began to detach and drop among the sticks of dynamite at his feet as Paulette came up.

He threw up the lid of the trunk, hauled out that transmitter or receiver or whatever it was in there, swung it once against the boulder, and let it fall. It landed on another stick of dynamite. Paulette winced but made no move; she seemed to be in a trance. The left-hand door was still sagging open on one hinge. He caught it, swung it down, using it as its own fulcrum, and the bottom hinge tore out. He tossed it aside.

"Can we go back now?" Paulette asked, almost timidly.

"No. Go way up the hill there and hide. Don't show yourself to anybody until you see a car with police markings."

He threw up the lid of the steel box and lifted out one of the suitcases. "Just in case this thing burns," he said as he heaved it out of sight on the other side of the boulder.

It landed with a thud, and Paulette winced. "But—the acid?"

He grabbed out the other bag and tossed it. "There is no acid. It was only a bluff, to keep him from blowing it until we could get out." He waved. "Hide. Take cover."

"Wh-what are you going to do?"

He'd already lunged into the seat and was fastening the belt. He grinned, and she seemed almost to recoil. "I want Kessler," he said. "And I've got one more dirty trick, if it works."

He hit the ignition switch. Wheels spun, caught, the car lurched back on the road, the rod still sticking out on the right, and began to gather speed. She looked after it, her lips just moving as she whispered. "Berserk . . . berserk. . . ." She turned then and began to climb up the slope.

The canyon turned left just ahead. He made it on screeching tires. There was a clatter on his right as the rod struck something and bent back along the side of the car. The canyon ran straight ahead for nearly half a mile between steep walls with scarcely room for two cars to pass. He was doing seventy now. This was the place to do it, right here, if he still had time. Kessler would be hot on their trail, God only knew how far behind.

The road ran out of the canyon, climbing into rougher hills. There was a jeep track going up over a ridge to his left. He swung onto it, skidding, and went bounding up, rocks clattering against the underside of the car. At the top he could see most of the immense valley to the south of him and the three hills still somewhat west of south. And a plume of dust. He grinned again, the same wolfish grin that had startled Paulette Carmody. There he was.

The car was traveling eastward at high speed from the general area of the three hills, headed for the road they'd come up. The rifleman, whichever one he was, would be afoot. Kessler was going to pick him up, and they'd turn north in pursuit of their $2,000,000 and their unarmed victims.

Then he saw something else. Far to the south, miles beyond the other car, were more streamers of dust. Several cars, at least, and they seemed to be going flat out, headed north. He sighed in relief. Carroll had made it back to the highway.

Kessler had turned north now, along the road they'd come up. When the car came abreast the low ridge where the rifleman had been, he could see it slow and stop for an instant, though it was too far to see the man himself. Then it came on, doing seventy at least, still miles ahead of the cars to the south.

He looked left along the ridge and the canyon below it. It would be a quarter mile at least till he'd be above the narrowest part of it, a rock-strewn demolition course, gullied, grown up with cactus, blocked by boulders, with no road at all. A jeep could make it, or anything with high clearance and four-wheel drive, but could this thing? He grinned again as he swung the wheel over and gunned it off the jeep track. There wouldn't be much of it left, but then there wouldn't be much left anyway.

He plowed through prickly pear, smashed the windshield on a limb of a dead tree, got stuck in loose gravel but made another run at it and got through, and tore two fenders off as he caromed off boulders, and then a hundred yards short of his objective there was a crunch underneath from a rock too high to clear. He looked back and saw a black line of oil. He'd punctured the pan, and the motor was going to freeze up any minute. He looked down and to his left. This would do.

The narrow canyon was below him, some three hundred feet down a fifty-degree slope. Kessler was still in the flat a mile away, approaching the entrance at seventy miles an hour. Still far back, the other plumes of dust were rising in pursuit, but gaining little if at all. He turned, stopped the car on the brink, and held it with the brake while he unfastened the belt. Kessler went out of sight at the upper end; then he was skidding around the turn into the narrow, half-mile straightaway below him. He released the brake, held the wheel while the car picked up momentum, headed it straight down, and jumped.

Romstead replaced the phone and picked up his drink. Mayo stood looking moodily out the window at the East Bay lights in the gathering dusk. He went over to her.

"That was Brubaker," he said. "I asked him to call and reverse the charges. They found him this afternoon. Out at the old Van Sickle place."

"Found whom?" she asked.

179

"You remember. Top Kick—that is, Delevan—said the old man killed one of them—"

"And the only reason you didn't kill two more is that the police got there in time to stop you. The strain is improving."

"Damn it, Mayo—."

"In another two or three generations I see a sort of super-Romstead, capable of wiping out whole communities."

"Look, if you have to fight me, at least be fair about it and stick to the facts. I wasn't trying to kill them. I was trying to get them out of the wreck before it burned. There was gasoline all over it—"

"And the dams don't even seem to matter," she went on, as if she hadn't even heard him. "They're only the receptacles, like the glass jars in *Brave New World*. Plant the seed anywhere, in a gently raised and civilized young Andalusian girl from Havana descended from five generations of university professors, and it germinates like dragon's teeth and comes clawing its way out of the womb one hundred percent Romstead, impervious to all other genes, to any distaff-inherited tendencies toward civilization at all—"

He sighed. He'd been through these things before; the only thing to do was heave to and ride it out. Keep your ass down, or as the bureaucrats put it nowadays, maintain a low profile.

"Mrs. Carmody said that while you were throwing that dynamite around like confetti and tearing the car apart with your bare hands, even she was afraid of you, and you were on her side."

The police had most of the facts now. Tex actually was from Texas, a fringe-area rodeo performer named Billy Heard who'd done federal time for narcotics smuggling along the border below El Paso. It was in prison that he met Kessler. The two of them, plus the girl named Debra and the man whose body Brubaker had found this afternoon, had planned the kidnapping of his father.

Jeri Bonner's only part in it was to find out where his money was and how much there was of it. She'd agreed to it, but reluctantly, because a fifty-dollar habit had already driven her to shoplifting and occasional prostitution and now, finally, to desperation, but she didn't know they planned to kill him, too. He, for his part, didn't know she was on heroin, and they were sleeping together when he was in San Francisco. Romstead had never had much faith in Mrs. Carmody's dictum that his father wouldn't have anything to do with a girl that young. The old stud would take a hack at any girl who was willing and that pretty, provided she was of legal age. He was good to her, and she liked him, so presumably she hadn't bungled when she brought back only the first page of the three-page stock listing. She'd just hoped the others would never find out.

Then, when she learned they'd killed him, she began to go to pieces. She ran for Coleville. Kessler by this time had found out too that she'd double-crossed them in the matter of the stocks. This, plus the fact they were now afraid she'd crack up completely and spill the whole thing to the police, had got her killed. Heard had done it, and he was the rifle expert who'd killed Lew Bonner after Bonner received Debra's letter addressed to Jeri and started an investigation of his own. It was Delevan—Top Kick—who'd been following Bonner around San Francisco that day.

Delevan had joined them by now in the planned big score, the kidnapping of Mrs. Carmody and himself, which was the reason their intelligence operations had improved to such an extent. He was a private investigator, and a good one until he began to itch for the bigger money. He replaced the one his father had killed, a man on whom the police didn't have much of a line as yet except that his name was Croft.

There'd been no telephone out at the Van Sickle place, of course, and they couldn't very well take him to a motel to make that first call to the bank, so they'd simply brought him back home. In their pickup camper, at night so they wouldn't be seen entering or leaving the place. They'd put the camper in the garage, forced him to make the phone call the next day, and stayed there until late at night again to leave. It was during this time that his father had killed Croft.

He was in his own bedroom, gagged, his wrists and ankles bound with tape. They'd been a little slipshod and careless about it, at least until he taught them better, so he was able to break the inadequate bindings on his wrists. But before he could free his ankles, Croft came in to check him. Apparently his father had heard him coming and had replaced his hands behind his back. Croft, however, had leaned over him to see for sure, which was the last mistake he ever made in a life presumably full of them. He never uttered a sound, but the final death tattoo of his feet kicked over a chair that brought the others. They took him back and buried him in a remote corner of the Van Sickle ranch.

They hadn't caught the girl yet, the oversexed chick in the next room, and nobody, so far, had copped out on what had happened to Debra. Romstead wasn't sure, nor were the police, why Debra had hidden a deck of junk in the old man's car out at the Van Sickle place, but it seemed likely that Heard, whose girl she was, was taking the stuff away from her when he caught her with it. He only smuggled the stuff; he detested the people who were stupid enough to use it.

Carroll Brooks was all right, recovering nicely in a San Diego hospital from a gunshot wound through the thigh. And the police so far had run down two hundred and fifteen thousand of the two hundred and fifty thousand dollars stashed in several safe-deposit boxes in San Francisco. They were hopeful of finding more.

"She was watching you—Mrs. Carmody, I mean—and hoping the police would get there in time herself. Standing there on the wreckage of one car with the second car balanced on top of it and teetering and ready to fall on you any second, beating what was left of the windshield out with a rock to get at the two men inside and kill them—"

She was running down now, he thought fondly, beginning to sputter and go further into left field after new indictments. She knew as well as he did, from the police reports, that Kessler and Heard were unconscious in there, and pretty soon she'd have to start looking for a way out of accusing him of wanting to kill two helpless and unconscious men who might already be bleeding to death anyway. So she'd demand to know if he'd intended to kill Kessler if he'd been on his feet and armed.

And he'd lie to her, as he had so much already, and tell her that of course he hadn't. If he didn't lie, he'd lose her, and he didn't think he could face that. He needed her. She seemed to be the only human being he'd ever really needed in his life.